"I am not an actress

"I can't make this eng⟨...⟩ ⟨...⟩lievable. I won't be the only one who finds our decision to marry a total farce."

She reached for the door as if to end the conversation on that note.

He reached for her, bracketing her with his arms. Stopping her from exiting the vehicle.

"No one is going to doubt that you have my attention." The space around them seemed to shrink. He noticed she remained very, very still. "That much is going to be highly believable."

She swallowed hard.

"Do you believe me, Adelaide?" He wanted to hear her say it. Maybe because it had been a long time since someone questioned his word. "Or shall I prove it?"

Her eyes searched his. Her lips parted. In disbelief? Or was she already thinking about the kiss that would put an end to all doubts?

"I believe you," she said softly, her lashes lowering as her gaze slid away from his.

* * *

His Secretary's Surprise Fiancé is part
of the Bayou Billionaires series—
Secrets and scandal are a Cajun family legacy
for the Reynaud brothers!

Dear Reader,

I've been a football fan since high school. To my classmates, I might have looked like a standoffish sort of girl (a clue to my future as an author, since writers are well-known for watching the action from the sidelines). Yet I was secretly enamored with football and the boys who played it.

There's something transformative about playing football together, apparently. I could see it in the friendships that football created. Football crosses socioeconomic boundaries and torches the usual cliques that form in high school. On the field and off, the players are family and brothers in arms. They back each other up. They pick each other up. They boost one another's spirits on the sidelines. There's an all-for-one and one-for-all dynamic on a football team that is truly inspirational.

Since high school, I've gone on to cheer for many other teams from the pros to Pop Warner. I've loved seeing my sons play and benefit from the way the game creates lifelong friendships. On autumn Sundays, our family spends quality time together watching the pros play on television or occasionally in person. In the Bayou Billionaires, it was important to me that we delivered this unsung side of the football world—the family created by the team. In the case of the Reynaud brothers, they are bound by blood, too. But what connects them most is their love of the game, a legacy they've each chosen for themselves.

I hope you enjoy meeting the Reynauds and seeing the other side of football, too!

Happy reading,

Joanne Rock

HIS SECRETARY'S SURPRISE FIANCÉ

—

JOANNE ROCK

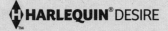

HARLEQUIN® DESIRE

Recycling programs
for this product may
not exist in your area.

ISBN-13: 978-0-373-73449-8

His Secretary's Surprise Fiancé

Printed in U.S.A.

www.Harlequin.com

While working on her master's degree in English literature, **Joanne Rock** took a break to write a romance novel and quickly realized a good book requires as much time as a master's program itself. Today, Joanne is a frequent workshop speaker and writing instructor at regional and national writer conferences. She credits much of her success to the generosity of her fellow writers, who are always willing to share insights on the process. More important, she credits her readers with their kind notes and warm encouragement over the years for her joy in the writing journey.

Books by Joanne Rock

Harlequin Desire

Bayou Billionaires

His Secretary's Surprise Fiancé

Harlequin Blaze

Double Play
Under Wraps
Highly Charged!
Making a Splash
Riding the Storm
One Man Rush
Her Man Advantage
Full Surrender
My Double Life

Visit the Author Profile page at Harlequin.com, or joannerock.com, for more titles!

To Catherine Mann, my longtime critique partner, for inviting me to dream up a Harlequin Desire series with her. We've brainstormed many books together over the years, but this was a special treat since we both got to write them! Thank you, Cathy, for being a creative inspiration and a wonderful friend.

One

Dempsey Reynaud would have his revenge.

Leaving the football team's locker room behind after losing the final preseason game, the New Orleans Hurricanes' head coach charged toward the media reception room to give the mandatory press conference. Today's score sheet was immaterial since he'd rested his most valuable players. Not that he'd say as much in his remarks to the media. But he would make damn sure the Hurricanes took their vengeance for today's loss.

They would win the conference title at worst. A Super Bowl championship at best.

As a second-year head coach on a team owned by his half brother, Dempsey had a lot to prove. Being a Reynaud in this town came with a weight all its own. Being an illegitimate Reynaud meant he'd been on a mission to deserve the name long before he became obsessed with bringing home a Super Bowl title to the Big Easy. A championship season would effectively answer his detractors, especially the sports journalists who'd declared that hiring him was an obvious case of favoritism. The press didn't understand his relatives at all if they didn't know that his older brother, Gervais, would be the first one calling for his head if he didn't deliver results. The Reynauds hadn't gotten where they were by being soft on each other.

More important, his hometown deserved a championship. Not for the billionaire family who'd claimed him as their own when he was thirteen. He wanted it for people who hungered for any kind of victory in life. For people who struggled every day in places like the Eighth Ward, where he'd been born.

Just like his assistant, Adelaide Thibodeaux.

She stood outside the media room about five yards ahead of him, smiling politely at a local sportswriter. When she spotted Dempsey, she excused herself and walked toward him, heels clicking on the tile floor like a time clock on overdrive. She wore a black pencil skirt with gold pinstripes and a sleeveless gold blouse that echoed the Hurricanes' colors and showed off the tawny skin of her Creole heritage. Poised and efficient, she didn't look like the half-starved ragamuffin who'd been raised in one of the city's toughest neighborhoods. The one who used to stuff half her lunch in her book bag to share with him on the bus home since he wouldn't eat again until the free breakfast at school the next morning. A lot had changed for both of them since those days.

From her waist-length dark hair that she wore in a smooth ponytail to her wide hazel eyes, framed by dark brows and lashes, she was a pretty and incredibly competent woman. The only woman he considered a friend. She'd been his assistant through his rise in the coaching ranks, her salary paid by him personally. As a Reynaud, he wrote his own rules and brought all his resources to the table to make a success of coaching. He'd been only too glad to create the position for her as he'd moved from Atlanta to Tampa Bay and then—two years ago—back to their hometown after his older brother, Gervais, had purchased the New Orleans Hurricanes.

There was a long, proud tradition of nepotism in football from the Harbaughs to the Grudens, and the Reynaud family was no different. They'd made billions in the global shipping industry, but their real passion was football. An obsession with the game ran in the blood, no matter how much some local pundits liked to say they were dilettantes.

"Coach Reynaud?" Adelaide called to him down the narrow hallway draped in team banners. Her use of his title alerted him that she was annoyed, making him wonder if that sportswriter had been hassling her. "Do you have a moment to meet privately before you take the podium?"

She handed him note cards, an old-fashioned preference at media events so he could leave his phone free for updates. He planned to brief the journalists on his regular-season roster, one of the few topics that would distract sports hounds from grilling him about today's loss in a preseason contest that didn't reflect his full team weaponry.

"Any last-minute emergencies?" He frowned. Adelaide had been with him long enough to know he didn't stick around longer than necessary after a loss.

He needed to start preparing for their first regular-season game. A game that counted. But he recognized a certain stiffness in her shoulders, a tension that wouldn't come from a defeat on the field even though she hated losing, too. She'd mastered hiding her emotions better than he had.

"There is one thing." She wore an earbud in one ear, the black cord disappearing in her dark hair; she was probably listening for messages from the public relations coordinator already in the media room. "It will just take a moment."

Adelaide rarely requested his time, understanding her job and his needs so intuitively that she could prepare weeks of his work based on little more than his daily texts or CCing her on important emails. If she needed to speak with him privately—now—it had to be important.

"Sure." He waved her to walk alongside him. "What do you need?"

"Privately, please," she answered tightly, setting off alarms in his head.

Commandeering one of the smaller offices along the hallway, Dempsey flicked on a light in the barren, generic space. The facilities in the building were nothing like the team headquarters and training compound in Metairie, where the Reynauds had invested millions for a state-of-the-art home. They played here because it was downtown and easier for their fans. The tiny box where they stood now was a fraction the size of his regular work space.

"What is it?" He closed the door behind him, sealing them inside the glorified cubicle with a cheap metal desk, a corded phone from another decade and walls so thin he could hear the lockers slamming and guys shouting in the team room next door.

"Dempsey, I apologize for the timing on this, but I can't put it off any longer." She tugged the earbud free, as if she didn't want to hear whatever was going on at the other end of her connection. "I've tried to explain before that I couldn't be a part of this season but it's clear I'm not getting through to you."

He frowned. What the hell was she talking about? When had she asked for a break? If she wanted vacation time, all she had to do was put it on his calendar.

"You're going to do this now?" He prided himself on control on the field and off. But after today's loss, this topic was going to test his patience. "Text me the dates you want off, take as long as you need to recharge and we'll regroup later. You're invaluable to me. I need you at full speed. Take care of yourself, Adelaide."

He turned to leave, ready to get back to work and relieved to have that resolved. He had a press conference to attend.

She darted around him, blocking the door with her five-foot-four frame. "You aren't listening to me now. And you haven't been listening to me for months."

The team owned tackling dummies for practice that stood taller than Adelaide, but she didn't seem to notice that Dempsey was twice her size.

He sighed. "What did I not hear?"

"I want to start my own business."

"Yes. I remember that. We agreed you would draw up a business plan for me to review." He knew she wanted to start her own company. She'd mentioned it last winter. She'd said something about specializing in clothes and accessories for female fans. She hoped to grow it over time, eventually securing merchandising rights from the team with his support.

He worried about her losing the financial stability she'd fought so hard to attain and figured she would realize the folly of the venture after thinking it over. He thought he'd convinced her to reevaluate those plans when he'd persuaded her to return for the preseason. Besides, she excelled at helping him. She was an invaluable member of the administrative staff he'd spent years building, so that when he finally had the right football personnel on the field, he could ride that talent to a winning year.

That year had arrived.

"I've emailed my business plan to you multiple times." She folded her arms beneath her breasts, an unwelcome reminder that Adelaide was an attractive woman.

She was his friend. Friendships were rare, important. Sex was…sex. She was more than sex to him.

"Right." He swallowed hard and hauled his gaze upward to her hazel eyes. "I'll get right on reading that after the press conference."

"Liar," she retorted. "You're putting me off again. I can't force you to read it, any more than I can make you read the messages and emails from your former female companions."

She arched an eyebrow at him, her rigid spine still plastered to the door, blocking his exit. It had never pleased her that he'd asked her to handle things like that from his inbox. But he needed her help deflecting unhappy ex-girlfriends, preventing them from talking to the press and diverting public attention from the team to his personal life. Adelaide was good at that. At so many things. His life frayed at the edges when she wasn't around.

Plus, he was devoting every second possible to the task of building a winning team to secure his place in the Reynaud family. It wasn't enough that he bore his father's last name. As an illegitimate son, he'd always needed to work twice as hard to prove himself.

And Adelaide's efforts supported that goal. He was good at football and finances. Adelaide excelled at everything else. He'd been friends with her since he'd chased off some bullies who'd cornered her in a neighborhood cemetery when she was in second grade and he was in third. She'd been so grateful she'd insinuated herself into his world, becoming his closest friend and a fierce little protector in her own right. Even after the time when Dempsey's rich, absentee father had shown up in his life to remove him from his hardscrabble life in the Eighth Ward—and his mother—for good. His mom had given him up for a price. Adelaide hadn't.

"Then, I'll resume management of the personal emails." He knew he needed to deal with Valentina Rushnaya, a particularly persistent model he'd dated briefly. The more famous a woman, apparently, the less she appreciated being shuffled aside for football.

"You will have no choice until you hire a new assistant," Adelaide replied. Then, perhaps realizing that she'd pushed him, she gave him a placating smile. "Thank you for understanding."

Hire a new assistant? What the hell? Was she grandstanding for something, like a raise? Or was she actually serious about launching her business right now at the start of the regular season?

"I don't understand," he corrected her, trying to talk

reason into her. "You need start-up cash for your new company. Even without reading your plan, I know you'll be depleting the savings you've worked so hard for on a very long shot at success. Everyone likes an underdog but, Addy, the risk is high. You have to know that."

"That's for me to decide." Fierceness threaded through her voice.

He strove to hang on to his patience. "Half of all small businesses fail, and the ones that don't require considerable investment. Work for one more year. You can suggest a raise that you feel is equitable and I'll approve it. You'll have a financial cushion to increase your odds of growing the company large enough to secure those merchandising rights."

And he would have more time to persuade her to give up the idea. Life was good for them now. Really good. She was an integral part of his success, freeing him up to do what he did best. Manage the team.

The voices and laughter in the hallway outside grew louder as members of the media moved from the locker-room interviews to the scheduled press conference. He needed to get going, to do everything possible to keep their future locked in.

"Damn it, I don't want a raise—"

"Then, you're not thinking like a business owner," he interrupted. Yes, he admired her independence. Her stubbornness, even. But he couldn't let her start a company that would fail.

Especially when she could do a whole hell of a lot of good for her current career and for his team. For him. He didn't have time to replace her. For that matter, as his longtime friend who probably understood him better than anyone, Adelaide Thibodeaux was too good at her job to be replaced.

He reached around her for the doorknob. She slid over to block him, which put her ass right over his hand. A curvy little butt in a tight pencil skirt. Her chest rose with a deep inhale, brushing her breasts against his chest.

He. Couldn't. Breathe.

Her eyes held his for a moment and he could have sworn he saw her pupils widen with awareness. He stepped back. Fast. She blinked and the look was gone from her gaze.

"I'm grateful that working with you gave me the time to think about what I want to do with my life. I got to travel all over and make important contacts that inspired my new business." She gestured with her hands, and he made himself focus on anything other than her face, her body, the memory of how she'd felt pressed up against him.

He watched her silver bracelet glinting in the fluorescent lights. It was an old spoon from a pawnshop that he'd reshaped as a piece of jewelry and given to her as a birthday present back when he couldn't afford anything else. Why the hell did she still wear that? He tried to hear her words over the thundering pulse in his ears.

"But, Dempsey, let's be honest here. I did not attend art school to be your assistant forever, and I've been doing this far too long to feel good about it as a 'fill-in job' anymore."

He didn't miss the reference. He'd convinced her to work with him in the first place by telling her the position would just be temporary until she decided what to do with her art degree. That was before she'd made herself indispensable. Before he'd started a season that could net a championship ring and cement his place in the family as more than the half brother.

He'd worked too hard to get here, to land this chance to prove himself under the harsh media spotlight to a league that would love nothing more than to see him fail. This was his moment, and he and Adelaide had a great partnership going, one he couldn't jeopardize with wayward impulses. Winning wasn't just about securing his spot as a Reynaud. It was about proving the worth of every kid living hand-to-mouth back in the Eighth Ward, the kids who didn't have mystery fathers riding in to save the day and pluck them out of a hellish nightmare. If Dempsey couldn't use football to make a difference, what the hell had he worked so hard for all these years?

"You can't leave now." He didn't have time to hash this out. And he would damn well have his way.

"I'm going after the press conference. I told you I would come back for the preseason, and now it's done." Frowning, she twisted the bracelet round and round on her wrist. "I shouldn't have returned this year at all, especially if this ends up causing hard feelings between us. But I can send your next assistant all my files."

How kind. He clamped his mouth shut against the scathing responses that simmered, close to boiling over. He deserved better from her and she knew it.

But if she was going to see him through the press conference, he still had forty minutes to change her mind. Forty minutes to figure out a way to force her hand. A way to make her stay by his side through the season.

All he needed was the right play call.

"In that case, I appreciate the heads-up," he said, planting his hands on her waist and shuffling her away from the door. "But I'd better get this press conference started now."

Her eyes widened as he touched her, but she stepped aside, hectic color rising in her cheeks even though they'd always been just friends. He'd protected that friendship because it was special. She was special. He'd never wanted to sacrifice that relationship to something as fickle as attraction even though there'd definitely been moments over the years when he'd been tempted. But logic and reason—and respect for Adelaide—had always won out in the past. Then again, he'd never touched her the way he had today, and it was messing with his head. Seeing that awareness on her face now, feeling the answering kick of it in his blood, made him wonder if—

"Of course we need to get to the conference." She grabbed her earpiece and shoved it into place as she bit her lip. "Let's go."

He held the door for her, watching as she hurried up the hallway ahead of him, the subtle sway of her hips making his hands itch for a better feel of her. No doubt about it, she was going to be angry with him. In time, she would see he had her best interests at heart.

But he had the perfect plan to keep her close, and the ideal venue—a captive audience full of media members—to execute it. As much as he regretted hurting a friend, he also knew she would understand at a gut level if she knew him half as well as he thought she did.

His game was on the line. And this was for the win.

That went better than expected.
Back pressed to the wall of the jam-packed media

room, Adelaide Thibodeaux congratulated herself on her talk with Dempsey, a man whose name rarely appeared in the papers without the word *formidable* in front of it. She'd made her point, finally expressing herself in a way that he understood. For weeks now, she'd been procrastinating about having the conversation, really debating her timing, since there never seemed to be a convenient moment to talk to her boss about anything that wasn't directly related to Hurricane football or Reynaud family business. But the situation was delicate. She couldn't afford to alienate him, since she'd need his help to secure merchandising rights as her company grew. And while she'd like to think they'd been friends too long for her to question his support…she did.

Somewhere along the line they'd lost that feeling they had back in junior high when they'd sit on a stoop and talk for hours. Now it was all business, all the time. That didn't seem to bother Dempsey, who lived and breathed work. But she needed more out of life—and her friends—than that. So now she was counting down the minutes of her last day on the job as his assistant. Maybe, somehow, they'd recover their friendship.

She hated to leave the team. She loved the sport and excelled at her job. In fact, she'd grown to enjoy football so much she couldn't wait to start her own high-end clothing company catering to female fans. The work married her love of art with her sports savvy, and the projected designs were so popular online she'd crowd funded her first official offering last week. She was ready for this next step.

And she was very ready for a clean break from Dempsey.

Her eyes went to him in the bright spotlight on the

dais where coaches and a few key players would take
turns fielding questions. The sea of journalists hid behind cameras, voice recorders and lights, a wall of de-
vices all currently aimed at Dempsey Reynaud, the
hard-nosed coach and her onetime friend who'd unknow-
ingly crushed most of her dreams for the past decade.

He was far too handsome, rich and powerful. Dempsey
might not ever see himself as fully accepted into the family, but the rest of the world breathed his name with the
same awe as they did the names of the other Reynaud
brothers. All four of them had been college football stars,
with the youngest two opting for NFL careers while the
older two had stepped into front-office roles in addition
to their work in the family's business empire. Each remained built like Pro Bowl players, however. Dempsey's
broad shoulders tested the seams of his Hurricanes jersey, his strong biceps apparent as he leaned forward at
the podium to provide his perspective on the game and
give an injury report.

With his dark brown hair and eyes a bit more golden
than brown, there was no mistaking Dempsey's rela-
tion to his half brothers. But the cleft in his chin and
the square jaw were all his own, his features sharp, his
mouth an unforgiving slash. He spoke faster, too, with
his stronger Cajun accent.

Not that she'd spent an inordinate amount of time cat-
aloging every last detail about the man she'd swooned
over as a teen. There was a time she would have done
backflips to make him notice her as more than just his
scrawny, flat-chested pal. But the only time she'd succeeded? He'd ended up noticing her as a tool for increasing his business productivity. He had honestly once
referred to her in those exact terms. He hadn't even

noticed when she'd ceased being much of a friend to him—forgoing personal exchanges in favor of taking care of business.

That hurt even more than not being noticed as a woman.

"Adelaide?" The voice of the PR coordinator sounded in her earpiece, a woman who had quickly seen the benefits of a coach with a personal assistant, unlike some of the front-office personnel in other cities where she'd worked. "I'm receiving calls and messages for Dempsey from Valentina Rushnaya. She's threatened to give some unflattering interviews if she can't arrange for a private meeting with him."

Adelaide's skin chilled. Dempsey's latest supermodel. The woman had been rude to Adelaide, unwilling to accept that her affair with Dempsey was over despite the extravagant diamond bracelet he'd sent as a breakup gift. Occasionally, Adelaide felt bad for the women he dated. She understood how it hurt to be kept at a distance after experiencing what it felt like to be the center of his attention—if only briefly. But she had no such empathy for Valentina.

Stepping to the back of the room, Adelaide spoke softly into her microphone, momentarily tuning out of the press conference as Dempsey wound up his opening remarks.

"I talked to Dempsey about this and he's agreed to handle it." She didn't see any need to share her plans to vacate her position. "Anything she says would either be old news, or blatant lies."

"Should we schedule a meeting to come up with a response plan, just in case?" Carole pressed. The woman stood on the far end of the room, her arms crossed in her navy power suit that was her daily uniform, her blond bob as durable as any helmet in the league. "Dempsey's new charity has their first major fund-raiser slated for next week. I think he'll be disappointed if this woman succeeds in deflecting any attention from that."

Adelaide would be equally disappointed.

The Brighter NOLA foundation had been her idea as much as his, a youth violence prevention initiative where Dempsey could leverage his success and influence to help some of the more gang-ridden communities in New Orleans. Like where they'd grown up. Or, more accurately, where he'd lived briefly and where she'd been stuck after he got out.

She'd had her own run-ins with youth violence.

"I'll make sure that doesn't happen." She would honor those words, even if it meant communicating with Dempsey after she walked away from the Silver Dome today. "She signed a strict nondisclosure agreement before she started dating Dempsey, so going to the press will be a costly move for her."

Dempsey had communicated as much to Adelaide in a one-line email when she'd mentioned it to him two weeks ago. He'd typed, She has no legal recourse, and attached a copy of the confidentiality agreement the woman had signed as part of his megaromantic dating procedure. In Adelaide's softer-hearted moments, she recognized that the single life could be difficult for an extraordinarily wealthy and powerful man in the public eye. He had to be practical. Careful. But the nondisclosure agreement, complete with enforcement clause and confidentiality protection, seemed over-the-top.

Given the number of women who still lobbied to be in his life, however, it must not deter many.

"Valentina is wealthier than some of the ladies he's dated," Carole pointed out. "But I hope she's just stirring trouble with us and not—" She stopped speaking suddenly and leaned forward. "Wait. Did he just say he has a personal announcement? What is he doing?"

From across the room, Adelaide noticed all of the PR coordinator's focus was on the lectern where Dempsey was facing down the media.

The audience sat in stillness, making her wonder what she'd missed. In the hushed moment, Dempsey held the room captive as always, but more anticipation than usual pinged through the crowd. She could see it in their body language, as the journalists sat straighter in their seats, all dialed in to whatever it was the Hurricanes' head coach was about to say.

"I got engaged today." He announced it as matter-of-factly as if he'd just read the latest update on a linebacker's injury report.

Murmurs of surprise rippled through the crowd of sportswriters while Adelaide reeled with shock. Engaged?

The floor seemed to shift beneath her feet. She reached behind her, searching for something to steady herself. He'd never mentioned an engagement. Her chest hurt with the weight of how little he trusted her. How little he cared about their old friendship. How much this new betrayal hurt, to not even know the most basic detail of his personal life—

"To my personal assistant," he continued, his gaze landing on her. "Adelaide Thibodeaux."

Two

Adelaide reeled back on her high heels.

Dempsey had just publicly declared an engagement. To her.

The man who was so cautious about every aspect of his personal life. The man who trusted her never to betray him even though he'd betrayed her in a million little ways over the years. How could he?

In her ear, Adelaide heard Carole squeal a congratulations. A few other members of the press who knew her—women, mostly, who were still vastly outnumbered in the football community—turned around to acknowledge her. Or maybe just study her to see what renowned bachelor Dempsey Reynaud would find appealing in the very average and wholly unknown Adelaide Thibodeaux.

Of course, the answer was obvious. She had no appeal other than the fact that Dempsey didn't want her to leave the team. And he was a man who always got his way.

She'd naively thought she could just turn her back on her job as his assistant and start a company that would rely upon good relations with the Hurricanes and the league in general for securing merchandising rights down the road. Something she couldn't afford to jeopardize if she wanted her company to be a success.

If she stood up and challenged him, she'd lose team support instantly. She didn't dare contradict him. At least not publicly. And no question, Dempsey absolutely knew that, as well.

Realization settled in her gut as smoothly and firmly as a sideline pass falling into a wide receiver's hands. She'd been outflanked and outmaneuvered by the smartest play caller in the game.

Her brand-new fiancé.

She needed time to think and regroup before she faced him and blurted out something she would regret. Adelaide darted out of the press conference just as a reporter began quizzing Dempsey about the quarterback's thumb. She didn't know what else to do. She lacked Dempsey's gift for complicated machinations that ruined other peoples' lives in the blink of an eye. Storming off was the best she could come up with to relay her displeasure and give herself time to think.

She tore off her earpiece even though Carole currently informed her she needed to stick around the building for any follow-up interviews.

Like hell.

Adelaide picked up her pace, heels grinding out a frantic rhythm on the concrete floor as she burst through a metal door leading to the stairwell. She headed down a flight to the custodial level of the dome, taking the route where she was least likely to encounter media.

The sports journalists hadn't really known what to do with the story about the Hurricanes' coach getting married. Sure—they would recognize the news value. But in that he-man room full of sports experts, no one would quiz the tersest coach in the league about his love life. They would hand that off to the social pages.

Who, in turn, would eat it up. All four of the Reynaud brothers had been in *People* magazine's Sexiest Men Alive list for two years running. The national media would be covering Dempsey's engagement, too. While she ran away.

She stumbled as her heel broke on the bottom step because her shoes were meant for work, not sprints. Hobbled, she shoved through the door on the ground level just as her phone started vibrating in her bag. She ignored it, trying to think of the most discreet way to reach her car two floors up.

A car engine rumbled nearby. It was the growl of a big SUV—a familiar SUV that slowed as it neared her. Dempsey's Land Rover, although it had probably never been operated by the owner himself.

Evan, his driver, lowered the tinted passenger window. He could have passed for a gangster with his shaved head, heavily inked chest and arms and frightening number of face piercings; his appearance gave Evan an added advantage in his dual role serving as personal security for their boss.

"Miss Adelaide," he said, even though she'd told him a half dozen times it made her feel like a kindergarten teacher when he called her that. "Do you need a ride?"

"Thanks, Evan," she huffed, out of breath more from runaway emotions than the mad dash out of the dome. "My car is on the C level, if you don't mind bringing me up there."

Relief washed through her as she limped over to the side of the vehicle. Before she could get there, Evan jumped out the passenger side and jogged around to help her, all two hundred sixty-four pounds of him. Before he blew out a knee, he'd been a top prospect on the Hurricanes' player roster, one she knew by heart.

She'd worked so hard to impress Dempsey over the years, memorizing endless facts and organizing mountains of information to help him with his job.

Only to be rewarded like this—by having him ignore her notice of resignation, refuse to discuss her concerns and announce a fake engagement to the very industry whose respect her future work depended upon.

"No problem." Evan tugged open the door and gave her a hand up into the passenger area of the vehicle specially modified to be chauffeur driven, complete with privacy screen. "Happy to help."

She waited for his knowing grin, certain he'd been listening to the press conference in the garage, but his face gave nothing away, eyes hidden behind a pair of aviator shades.

"I appreciate it." She tried to smile even though her voice sounded shaky. "I parked on the west side today. Close to the elevators."

Ticket holders had cleared out after the game, leaving the lot mostly empty now, save for a few hardcore fans that stuck around for autographs. The press parking area was separate, three floors up.

"Got it." Evan shut the door with a nod and she settled into the perforated leather seats. The bespoke interior was detailed with mother-of-pearl and outfitted with multiple viewing screens that Dempsey used to watch everything from game film to feeds from foreign stock exchanges to keep up with the Reynauds' family shipping business in the global markets.

Sadly, she knew the stats of most of the ships, too.

Her phone continued to vibrate in her bag, a hum against her hip where her purse rested, a reminder that her life had just fallen apart. Squeezing her eyes shut, she felt the Land Rover glide into motion and wished she could seize the wheel and simply keep driving far, far away from here. As if there was anywhere out of reach of the Reynauds, she thought bitterly.

Out of habit, she touched her right hand to the bracelet on her left wrist to feel the smooth metal that Dempsey had heated and shaped into a special present for Adelaide's twelfth birthday. The jewelry was worth far more than any of the identical diamond parting gifts he'd doled out to lovers over the years. Maybe she'd been foolish to see so much meaning in those years they'd spent together when his life had gone on to change so radically. She'd always thought she would do anything for him.

But not at this price. Not when he stopped being her friend and started thinking he was the boss of every aspect of her life. He couldn't dictate her career moves.

Or her choice of fiancé, for crying out loud. The funny part was, there had been a time in her life when she would have traded anything to hear him announce their engagement. But she'd grown up since the days she'd harbored those schoolgirl hopes. Once his father's limo had arrived to take him out of her world and into the rarefied air of the Reynaud family compound in Metairie, things had never been quite the same between them. Sure, he'd checked up on her now and then when the family was in Louisiana and not one of their other homes around the globe. Yet he always seemed acutely aware of the expectations of his family, and they did not include hanging out with a girl from the old neighborhood. For that matter, Dempsey had put all his considerable drive into becoming a true family heir, increasing his workload at school and throughout college. Eventually, he'd dated women in his same social circles, and Adelaide had remained just a friend.

Peering out the dark tinted windows, she noticed that Evan had exited onto the wrong floor of the parking garage. She reached for the communications panel to buzz him even as the SUV slowed by the east side elevators a floor below where she needed to be.

"Evan?" she said aloud when he didn't answer right away. "Can you hear me?"

"Yes, Miss Adelaide?" His voice sounded different. Sheepish?

Maybe he knew he'd made a mistake.

"We're in the wrong spot—"

She stopped when the elevator doors opened. Dempsey strode out, a building security guard on either side of him.

"Sorry, ma'am. The boss called."

Of course Evan hadn't made a mistake. He'd come here to pick up the man who called all the shots. Or had he been sent downstairs earlier to retrieve her? Either way, she was screwed. Her escape plan was over before she'd even gotten it off the ground.

At almost the same time, the stairwell door opened

and a small throng of reporters raced out, camera lights spearing into the parking garage gloom as they shouted Dempsey's name and called out follow-up questions he must not have addressed in the televised press conference.

"Coach Reynaud, have you set a wedding date?"

"How do you think this will affect your team?"

"How long have you been dating your assistant?"

The last question came from a thin woman who reached him first, her voice recorder shoved toward his face. One of the security guards warded her off easily enough, opening the door of the Land Rover so Dempsey could step up into the vehicle.

"Does Valentina know?" the skinny reporter shouted, banging on the window of the SUV as Dempsey closed the door and locked it behind him.

Adelaide scooted to the far end of the seat as he lowered himself beside her, the soft leather cushion shifting beneath her as the vehicle started into motion again.

"Hello, Adelaide." He made the greeting sound like so much more than it was, his deep voice tripping along her senses the way it sometimes did when he used her whole name.

She hated that he could inspire those feelings even now. It was as if he'd sucked all the air out of the small space so she couldn't catch her breath. She watched in silence as he tugged off his team jersey, tossing the Hurricanes gear onto the opposite seat and leaving him clad in a simple black silk T-shirt with his black pants. He looked like a very hot hit man.

A hit man who'd targeted her business. Her future. All for his own selfish ends.

"Can you call Evan and remind him my car is on

the C level?" She glared at him, reminding herself with every breath not to get too emotional. Not to let all the anger fly, as much as she wanted to do just that.

She'd seen him in action for years, knew him well enough to understand that no one won battles with him by acting on feelings. Dempsey ran right over adversaries who couldn't negotiate with the benefit of cool reason.

"It might not be wise to drive when you're angry." He set aside his phone and stretched an arm along the back of the seat.

Almost touching her. Not quite.

Not the way he had back in that vacant office before the press conference when she'd inserted herself between him and the door. When she'd felt the warmth of his hand on her hip. Brushed up against him chest to chest in a moment that had almost caused cardiac arrest. She swallowed hard and refused to think about all that wayward attraction, which had always been one-sided.

"It might not be wise to kidnap the assistant you're dating either." She couldn't keep the bitterness out of her voice.

"We're not dating. We're engaged." He reached to tug a lock of her hair, as easily as if she still had pigtails. As if she would still follow him anywhere just because he said so. "I'll send someone back for your car later. It will be safer to stick together."

"Safer for who exactly?" She tried not to wrench away from him, would not let him see how much this cavalier treatment got under her skin. Even now, despite the anger inside, another heat simmered right along with it. "And who made you lord of what I can and can't do? Turn the damn car around."

Being trapped beside his powerful presence in the back of a private luxury vehicle only stirred to life those other potent feelings she'd tried so hard to stamp out long ago.

"I don't think either of us wants to create a firestorm around the team right now," he reminded her.

"Seriously? Which is why you chose to announce an engagement to the press when you knew I couldn't contradict you." She clenched her fingers tight and contained her temper as Evan drove the SUV out of the parking garage and into the early-evening traffic heading west, away from her home.

Toward the Reynauds' private compound in Metairie. She didn't need to ask where they were headed, any more than Evan needed to ask. The world simply moved according to Dempsey's wishes.

"I realize you think I did this just for me. For the team. But I did it for you, too." His golden-brown eyes remained on her even when the viewing screens built into the overhead console flipped to life with game updates from around the league.

Being the focus of his undivided attention had the power to rattle any woman.

"We've been friends for too long for you to trot out that kind of BS with me." She folded her arms tight across her chest, her body reacting all kinds of erratically around him today. "Can we at least be honest with each other?"

"I am being honest." He shifted in his seat, turning toward her. Moving closer. "Adelaide, I don't want to see you fail at anything. Ever. And I promise you, if you stick this out with me—just this one more season—I will ensure that your company gets off the ground with all the benefits of my connections."

It was a lot to promise her. Worth a heck of a lot more than those diamond bracelets he passed out like consolation prizes.

"I don't want a company that is a glorified Reynaud hand-off. I want the satisfaction of developing it myself." There had been a time when he would have understood that. "Don't you remember what it feels like to want to build something that is all your own? Without the benefit of—" she waved her arm to encompass his custom-detailed world in a vehicle that cost more than most people's homes "—all this?"

His phone rang before he could answer her. And worse?

He held up a hand to indicate that he needed to take it.

"Reynaud," he growled into the device.

Tuning him out, she fumed beside him. This was precisely why she needed to leave. She understood that he worked eighteen-hour days every day and that he took his business concerns as seriously as his team. But it had been too many years since he'd even pretended to make time for her or the friendship they'd once shared. He spoke to her as his assistant, not like the girl who had once been privy to all his secrets.

He had no idea about the strides she'd made in her business over the past few weeks—the way she'd pulled off funding for a short run of her first clothing item. He hadn't been there to applaud her unique efforts or otherwise acknowledge anything she did, and she was sick of it. Sick of his whole world that could never pause for one moment. Even for the conversation they'd been having.

By the time Dempsey disconnected his call, she could barely hold on to her temper.

Enough was enough.

Setting aside his phone after clearing up some problems in Singapore, where it was already Monday morning, Dempsey hoped the time-out from the confrontation with Adelaide had helped her to cool off and see his side. She sure had backed him into a corner by quitting out of the blue.

What else was he supposed to have done when she'd forced his hand like that? The engagement was simply a countermove.

"Adelaide," he began again, only to have her swing around in the seat to glower at him.

"How kind of you to remember we were in the middle of a conversation." Her clipped words suggested her temper wasn't anywhere close to cooling down. "Do you need a refresher on what we were discussing? One, our ridiculous engagement." She ticked off items on her fingers. "Two, your sneak attack of having Evan lying in wait for me in the garage so I couldn't make a clean break from the stadium today. Three, your inability to understand why I want to build my own company from the ground up, without the almighty Reynaud name behind me—"

"How can you, of all people, suggest I don't understand what it's like to want to develop your own company? To build your own team?" His voice hit a rough note even as his volume went softer. "You know why I went into coaching. Why it means everything to me to win a championship for this town."

He remembered shared rides home that weren't in the

back of a Land Rover. Shared rides in a cramped bus full of bigger, stronger kids who amped up their street cred by converting new gang members or beating the living crap out of nonconverts. Of course he knew. He was giving back with his foundation. Constructing a positive environment with the Hurricanes for a community that needed an identity. Creating a team to root for that wore football jerseys instead of gang colors.

Adelaide didn't answer, though. She stared at him with a stony expression. He didn't have a clue what she was thinking. When had he lost the ability to read her? His gaze dipped to her mouth, set in a stubborn line. He read that well enough. Although, after that brush up against her before the press conference, he suddenly found himself wondering what she'd taste like. He hadn't let himself think along those lines in years, always protecting their long-standing friendship. Something had gone haywire inside him after he'd touched her today. He couldn't write it off as passing awareness of her as a woman, the way he had a few times as a teen. This attraction had been fierce, making him question if he'd ever be able to see her as just a friend again. It rattled him. He'd grown to rely on her too much to have an affair go wrong.

And it would. Adelaide was not the kind of woman to have affairs, for one thing. For another? Dempsey only conducted relationships that came with an expiration date.

With an effort, he steered himself back to his point.

"I've got controlling shares in businesses around the globe," he reminded her as they got off I-10 and headed north toward Lake Pontchartrain. "But being CEO of this or vice president of that doesn't mean as much when it's handed to you. With coaching, it's different. I earned a spot in this league. I am putting my stamp on this team, and through it—this town. I'm creating that right now, with my own two hands."

He pulled his eyes away from her, needing a moment that wasn't filled with the distracting new view of her as more than just his friend. He did not want to think about Adelaide Thibodeaux's lips.

"You're right." She reached across the seat and touched his forearm. Squeezed lightly. "I'm upset about…a lot of things. But you deserve to be proud of your efforts with the team and with Brighter NOLA." Her hand fell away, briefly grazing his thigh.

Then she pulled back fast.

He wished he could will away his reaction just as quickly.

"I understand you're angry." Maybe that was the source of all this tension pinging back and forth. Passions were running high today between the team's loss, the start of the regular season and her trying to quit. "But let's hammer out a plan to get through it. You want to build your own business, fine. Just wait until after the season is over and I'll at least help you finance it. I can offer much better terms than the bank."

The moon hung low over the lake as the SUV wound around the side streets leading to the family's waterfront acreage. The lake was shallow here, requiring boat owners to install long docks to moor their watercraft. Dempsey couldn't recall the last time he'd taken a boat out, since all his time was devoted to football and business.

"That's very generous of you. But I can't stay a whole season." Briefly, she squeezed her temples between her thumb and forefingers. "I posted a design of my first shirt and won crowd funding for the production. I need to honor that commitment after my followers made it happen for me."

And he had missed that milestone, even if it was just enough capital for a small run of shirts and not the launch of an entire business. He admired that—how she'd started off things so conservatively that her potential buyers had bought the clothes before she'd even made them. She was smart. Savvy. All the more reason he needed her. He could help her with her business after she helped him solidify his.

"Congratulations, Addy. I didn't know about that. So give me four weeks." He did not want to compromise on this. But four weeks bought him more time to convince her to stay longer. To show her that she had a place with the team. "The deal still stands. I'll help you with the startup costs. You retain full control. But you will stay with me for another month to get the season underway."

"What about the engagement? What happens to that ridiculous fiction next month?"

"You can break it off for whatever reason you choose." He trusted her to be fair. He might not have been paying much attention to her for the past few years in his intense drive to lead his team, but he knew that much about her.

When the time came to "break up," she wouldn't drag him through a scandal the way Valentina had threatened. Especially since he and Adelaide would still be working together, because no way in hell was he losing her. Four weeks was a long time to win her over now that he understood how high the stakes were. A season like this might only come around once in a lifetime. If he didn't make the most of it and secure the championship now, he might never get another shot.

"And until then? What will your family think of this sudden news? Will you at least tell them the truth so we don't have to pretend around them?" She bit her lip as they drove through the gates leading to the Reynaud family acreage along the lake.

She'd never seemed at ease here, not from the first time she'd set foot on the property for his high school graduation party and spent most of the time searching for shells on the shore.

The SUV rolled past the mammoth old Greek Revival house where Dempsey had spent his teen years, now occupied by his older brother, Gervais. Henri and Jean-Pierre split an eleven-thousand-square-foot Italianate the family acquired when they'd bought out a former neighbor. Neither of them stayed with the family for long, since Henri and his wife had a house in the Garden District and Jean-Pierre spent the football season in New York with his team.

Dempsey's place was slightly smaller. He'd specially commissioned the design to repeat the Greek Revival style of the main house, with four white columns in the front, and a double gallery overlooking the lake in back.

Evan parked the vehicle in front, but Dempsey didn't open the door. "My family doesn't need to know the truth about our relationship." He reached for her hand to reassure her, guessing she would be bothered by the lie. "It will be simpler if we keep the details private."

Her hand closed around his for a moment, as though it was a reflex. As though they were still friends. But damned if he didn't feel that spark of awareness again.

Whatever had happened between them back at the stadium was not going away.

"Your family won't believe it." She shook her head. "We've kept things strictly platonic for too long to feel...*that* way."

She withdrew her hand from his. Either he was really losing his touch with women, or they'd both been feeling "that way" today. Was it the first time it had happened for her, or had she thought about him romantically in the past?

It bothered him how much he wanted to know.

"It's none of their business." He didn't care what anyone thought. His brothers were too caught up in their own lives to pay much attention to Dempsey outside of his work with the Hurricanes. He'd been the black-sheep brother ever since their father had shown up with him in tow as a scrawny thirteen-year-old. "The engagement is important, since Valentina threatened to cause trouble for the Brighter NOLA fund-raiser by going to the media with some story about my nondisclosure agreements. The announcement of my marriage to you trumps her ploy ten times over. No one will care about her story, let alone believe it."

"Ah. How convenient." Adelaide wrenched her purse onto her lap and started digging through it. Finding a tube of lip balm, she uncapped it, twisted the clear shiny wand upward and slicked it over her mouth until her lips glistened.

His own mouth watered. Then he recalled her words.

"It is useful." He watched her smooth her dark hair behind her ears, the primping a sure sign of nerves. "The engagement helps me to keep you close and prevents Valentina from sabotaging something you and I worked hard to develop. That foundation is too important for her to derail our efforts."

"Well, I don't find it useful. Or convenient." Adelaide's eyes flashed a brighter jade than normal, her cheeks pink with a hint of temper. "I am not an actress. I can't make an engagement believable to your family when they've hardly noticed me in all the time we've known each other."

"We can address that."

"If you think I'm going to start tossing my hair—" she exaggerated some kind of feminine hair fluffing "—or slinking around your house in skintight gowns to convince anyone that I'm the kind of female who could capture your attention..."

"You think that's what I notice in a woman?" He couldn't say if he felt more amused at her attempt to toss her hair, or dismayed that she perceived him as shallow.

Her shrug spoke volumes.

"Your challenge could not be clearer if you'd thrown a red flag on the field." Something stirred inside him— something deeper than the earlier flashes of attraction.

A bone-deep need to prove her wrong. He was not a shallow man. He'd simply dated women who could go into a romantic relationship with eyes wide-open. He refused to give any woman false expectations.

"I'm not challenging you." She bit her lip again, her shiny gloss fading as her anxiety spiked. "Simply pointing out what has historically intrigued you about the fair sex. I won't be the only one who finds our decision to marry a total farce."

She reached for her door handle as if to end the conversation on that note.

He reached for her, bracketing her with his arms. Stopping her from exiting the vehicle.

"No one is going to doubt that you have my attention." The space around them seemed to shrink. He noticed she remained very, very still. "That much is going to be highly believable."

She swallowed hard.

"Do you believe me, Adelaide?" He wanted to hear her say it. Maybe because it had been a long time since someone had questioned his word. "Or shall I prove it?"

Her eyes searched his. Her lips parted. In disbelief? Or was she already thinking about the kiss that would put an end to all doubts?

"I believe you," she said softly, her lashes lowering as her gaze slid away from his.

He had no choice but to release her then, his argument won. He should be relieved, since he didn't want to give Adelaide false expectations of their relationship. But as they exited the SUV and headed into the house, he couldn't help a twinge of disappointment that she hadn't challenged him on that last point, too.

He'd been all too ready to prove that the attraction he felt for her was one hundred percent real.

Three

Everything about this day felt off-kilter to Adelaide as she followed Dempsey up the brick steps onto the sprawling veranda of his house. Fittingly, she limped up the steps in her broken heel, unable to find her footing around him.

He'd commissioned the home when he'd first taken the head-coaching job in New Orleans, though it hadn't been completed until last spring. As if the Reynaud family complex hadn't been impressive enough before, now Dempsey's stalwart white mansion echoed the strong columns of the main house where he'd grown up. His place, just under ten thousand square feet, was only slightly less intimidating than Gervais's historic residence on the hill that had been built in the same style two centuries prior. She could see the rooftop from here, although the live oaks gave the structures considerable privacy. It helped to have the billions from Reynaud Shipping at their disposal, though the generations-old wealth was one of many reasons Adelaide had always felt out of place here.

Today, she had even more reason to feel off her game.

From the erratic pounding of her heart to the all-over tingle of awareness that lingered after their talk in the back of the Land Rover, she felt too dazed to don her usual armor of professionalism. What had he been thinking to focus that kind of sensual attention on her? She'd been so breathless when he'd bracketed her between those powerful arms, his chest just inches from her own, that she hadn't been able to think straight. Hadn't been able to question why they needed to enact this crazy charade for his family that had always intimidated her.

She slipped off her unevenly heeled shoes at the door and walked barefoot into his house. Once she shook off this fog of attraction, she would talk sense into Dempsey and leave. She'd wanted a clean break from him, and now he'd changed the playing field between them so radically she didn't know what to expect. Should she put her product launch on hold? Or should she keep fighting to end her commitment to the Hurricanes? She needed to sort through it all without the added confusion of this new sensual spark between them.

"You might remember from the blueprints that there's an extra bedroom upstairs and one downstairs." He led her through the wide foyer past a grand staircase. He used an app on his phone, she realized, to switch on lights and lower blinds as they moved through the space. "Both have en suite facilities. I can send Evan to your place to pick up some things for you when he retrieves your car."

They paused in an expansive kitchen at the back of the house, connecting to a dining area with floor-to-ceiling French doors that opened onto the yard overlooking the lake. There was another set of French doors in the family room, also accessing the back gallery and lawn. It was a perfect place for entertaining, although she would be surprised if Dempsey had hosted many people here. She certainly hadn't been invited to any private parties at his home even though she'd helped choose any number of fixtures and had spoken with his contractors more often than he had.

But in all fairness, Dempsey had always spent the majority of his time on the road or at the office. She doubted he'd spent many nights here himself.

"The house is beautiful," she said finally. "You must be pleased with how it turned out. I know I looked at the plans with you when you first approved the blueprints, but seeing the real thing… Wow."

She shook her head as she took in the ceiling medallions around matching chandeliers that were either imported antiques or had been designed by a master craftsman. The natural-stone fireplace in the kitchen gave that space warmth even when it wasn't lit, while another fireplace in the family room had a hand-carved fleur-de-lis motif that matched the ceiling medallions.

"Thank you. I haven't spent much time here, but I'm happy with it. Why don't I order some food and we can hash out a plan for the next few weeks while we eat?" He set his phone on the maple butcher-block top of the kitchen island, one of the elements of the house she'd helped choose, along with the appliances.

But when she'd been comparing kitchen options on her tablet, she'd simultaneously been investigating a wide receiver's shoulder injury and a competing team's new blitz packages. No wonder she'd all but forgotten the details until now.

"Anything is fine." She wasn't in the mood to eat, her body still humming with awareness and a sensual hunger of a more unsettling kind after those heated few moments earlier.

Even in this giant house, Dempsey's magnetic pull remained as potent as if they were separated by inches and not feet. When he walked toward her, her breath caught. Her heart skipped one beat. Then two. It had been one thing to ignore her reaction to him when he'd always treated her as a friend. But now that he'd opened that door to a different kind of relationship, teasing her with hints of the possible chemistry they might have together...her whole being seemed to spark and simmer with the possibilities. That kind of distraction would not make figuring out her professional life any easier.

First she needed to strategize a method for dealing with him and this fake engagement, then find a way out of the house as soon as possible. She couldn't survive spending twenty-four hours a day with him, especially when she wasn't sure if he genuinely felt some kind of attraction, too, or if he'd always known about the feelings she thought she'd kept well hidden. Would he be so cruel as to use that attraction now to his advantage?

"Gervais has a full-time chef at his place now that Erika is having twins." He gestured in the general direction of the house on the hill where his older brother had settled his soon-to-be wife, a beautiful foreign princess who would fit right into the Reynaud family. "It's easy to have something sent over."

"I'm too wound up to eat." She shrugged. "I would make some tea, though." She peered around the kitchen, not seeing a kettle or any other signs of basic staples.

"Tea." He typed in something on his phone and shook his head. "I'll ask for a few things." He set the device aside. "Evan will bring it over in half an hour or so. I'll show you the rooms so you can choose one. You'll be safer from the press here. You have to know that my family's security rivals that of Fort Knox."

The very last thing she wanted to do was choose a bedroom in Dempsey's house, especially when her pulse fluttered so erratically just to be near him. It didn't matter to her body that she was angry with him and his high-handed move. Some fundamental part of their relationship had shifted today; a barrier that she'd thought was firm had caved. She felt raw from having that defense ripped away.

He stalked through the family room into the western wing of the house and pushed open the door of an expansive bedroom with carpet and walls in blues and grays, a king-size modern bed with a pristine white duvet and a white love seat in front of yet another fireplace, this one with a gray granite surround.

The en suite bath on the far end of the room had a stone bathtub the size of a kiddie pool, spotlighted with an overhead pendant lamp on a dim setting. Gray cabinets and white marble were understated accents to the dominant tub.

"You didn't take this one for your room? I thought you had chosen that tub especially for you," she asked over his shoulder, realizing as she said it that she'd allowed herself to stand very close to him to better see the whole space. If she leaned forward just a little, she could rest her cheek against his back where broad shoulders tapered to a narrow waist.

It didn't help that she'd been thinking about him lounging in that huge custom tub, muscles glistening.

"The view is better from the suite upstairs." He turned to face her and it was all she could do not to scuttle backward. She did not need to have both Dempsey and a bed in her field of vision. "I'll show you the bedroom near mine."

"No. I mean—there's no need." She would sleep downstairs by herself if it meant they could end this tour faster. "I can sleep here tonight."

She wasn't committing to spending any more time than that in this house. One night was bad enough, but she had too much to work out with him to leave just yet.

"Are you sure you'll be all right alone down here?" He frowned. But then, he knew when they traveled she preferred a room close to his. Her house had been broken into as a teenager—after he'd moved away from her. And she felt jittery at night sometimes.

"I'm certain. Your family's security rivals Fort Knox. Remember?" She nodded, knowing she wouldn't sleep well under Dempsey's roof for entirely different reasons than that long-ago robbery where she'd hidden under her bed for half an hour after the thieves had left. "But you mentioned discussing a plan for the next few weeks?" She backed up a step now, out into the hallway away from the warmth of his broad shoulders. "I'll rest easier once we talk through this. Actually, if we can come up with a plan, I'll say good-night and leave you to watch your game film."

She knew his habits well. Understood how he spent most nights after a day on the field, watching the action on the big screen where he could replay mistakes over and over again, making notes for the next day's meetings so the team could begin implementing adjustments.

"Come upstairs first." He turned off the light and headed back toward the front of the house, where she remembered seeing the main staircase. "I want you to see my favorite part of this place."

Something in his voice—his eyes—made her curious. Maybe it was a hint of mischief, the same kind that had once led them into a haunted house, which turned out to be the coolest spot in their neighborhood after she got over being scared of the so-called voodoo curse on the place. Besides, she needed to see hints of her old friend—or even her boss—inside the very hot, very sexy male she kept seeing instead. So she focused on that "I dare you" light he'd had in his eyes as she padded up the dark mahogany stairs behind him, the two-story foyer a deep crimson all around them.

He'd come a long way from the apartment on St. Roch Avenue where he'd battled river rats as often as his mother's stream of live-in boyfriends, each one more of a substance abuser than the last. His mom had been a local beauty when she'd had an anonymous one-night stand with Dempsey's father after meeting at the restaurant where she'd waitressed. She hadn't read the papers enough to recognize Theo Reynaud, but when she'd seen him on television over a decade later, she'd remembered that one night and contacted him.

Adelaide hadn't been at all surprised when Dempsey's real father had shown up to claim him. She'd known as soon as she'd met Dempsey—way back when he'd saved her from a beat down in a cemetery where she'd gone to play—that he was destined for more than the Eighth Ward. In her fanciful moments, she'd imagined him as a prince and the pauper character like the fairy tale. He had the kind of noble spirit that his poor birth couldn't hide.

And even though she wanted to think she was destined for more than her tiny studio still a stone's throw from St. Roch Avenue, she was determined to make it happen because of her hard work and talents. Not because of all the wealth and might of Dempsey Reynaud.

"Through here." He waved her past the open door to another bedroom, the floor plan coming back to her now that she'd walked through the finished house. She recalled the two huge bedrooms upstairs and, down another hall, the in-law suite with a separate entrance accessible from outside above the three-car garage.

She didn't remember the den where he brought her now. But he didn't seem to be showing her the den so much as leading her through it to another doorway that opened onto the upstairs gallery. As he pushed open the door, moonlight spilled in, drawing her out onto the deep balcony with a woven mat on the painted wooden floor. A flame burst to life in the outdoor fireplace built into the exterior wall of the house, a feature he must have been controlling with the app on his phone. An outdoor couch and chairs surrounded the fireplace, but he led her past those to the railing, where he stopped. In front of them, Lake Pontchartrain shone like glass in the moonlight, a few trees swaying in a nighttime breeze making a soft swishing sound.

"I haven't spent much time here, but this is my favorite spot." He rested his phone and his elbows on the wooden railing, staring out over the water.

"If this was my house, I don't think I'd ever leave it."

There was so much to take in. Lights from Metairie and a few casino boats glittered at the water's edge. Long docks were visible like shadowy fingers reaching out into the lake, while the causeway spanned the water as far as she could see, disappearing to the north.

"I wish I had more free time to spend here, too." He turned to face her, his expression inscrutable in the moonlight. "But someone might as well make use of it. Move in for the next few weeks, Adelaide. Stay here."

Normally, Dempsey wouldn't have appreciated an interruption of a crucial conversation. But Evan's announcement of dinner had probably prevented another refusal from Adelaide, so he counted the disruption as a fortuitous break in the action.

Now they ate dinner in high-backed leather chairs in the den, watching highlights from around the league. They attempted to name the flavors in the naturalistic Nordic cuisine with ingredients specially flown in to appease Gervais's fiancée's pregnancy cravings. The white asparagus flavored with pine had been interesting, but Dempsey found himself reaching for the cayenne pepper to bring the flavor of Cajun country to the salmon. You could take the man out of the bayou, but apparently his palate stayed there. Dempsey's birth mother may have been hell on wheels, but before she'd spiraled downward from her addictions, she'd cooked like nobody's business.

"I can't believe you have Gervais's chef making meals like this for you." Adelaide took more asparagus, finding her appetite once she'd glimpsed the kind of food prepared by the culinary talent being underutilized by Gervais and his future wife. "That is another reason I could never live in this house. I'd weigh two tons if I could have dishes arrive at my doorstep with a phone call. What a far cry from takeout pizza."

"I think you're safe with asparagus." He'd always thought she'd eaten too little, even before he started training with athletes who calculated protein versus carb intake with scientific precision to maximize their workout goals.

His plan for dinner had been to keep things friendly. No more toying with the sexual tension in the air, in spite of how much that might tempt him. He needed Adelaide committed to his plan, not devising ways to escape him, so he would try to keep a lid on the attraction simmering between them.

For now.

If she moved into his house, he would spend more time here, too. He'd keep an eye on her over the next few weeks, solidify their friendship and learn to read her again. He'd taken her friendship for granted and he regretted that, but it wasn't too late to fix it. He'd find time to help her with her future business plans, all while convincing her to stick out the rest of the season.

"You don't understand." She pointed her fork at him. She'd put on one of his old Hurricanes T-shirts about six sizes too large for her, her dark hair twisted into a knot and held in place with a pencil she'd snagged off his desk. She still wore her black pencil skirt, but he could only see a thin strip of it beneath the shirt hem. "I peeked in the dessert containers while you were finding a shirt for me and I already gained twelve pounds just looking at the sweets. There is a crème brûlée in there that is…" She trailed off. "Indescribable."

"This you know just from looking?" He remembered how much she loved sweets. When they were growing up, he'd given her the annual candy bar he'd won each June for a year's worth of good grades. Now that he could have bought her her own Belgian chocolate house, though, he couldn't recall the last time he'd given her candy.

"I may have sampled some." She grinned unrepentantly. Then, as if she recalled whom she was talking to, her smile faded. "Dempsey, I can't stay here."

"Can't, or won't?"

"I've already told you that I don't want to pretend we are engaged in front of your family, and this puts me in close proximity to them every day," she reminded him. Then she pointed wordlessly to a screen showing a catch worthy of a highlight reel from one of the players they'd be facing in next Sunday's game. It was a play that he'd already heard about in the Hurricanes' locker room.

He admired how seamlessly Adelaide fit into his world. He'd had a tough time bridging the gap between life as a Reynaud and his underprivileged past, acting out as a teen and choosing to work his way up in the ranks as a coach rather than devote all his attention to the family business. But Adelaide never acted out.

Or at least, not until today.

"I saw that catch," he said, acknowledging her. "We'll definitely keep an eye on that receiver." Then, needing to focus on Adelaide, he shoved aside his empty plate. "But regarding staying in the house, you don't need to worry about my family. I will spend more time here, too, so I'll be the one to deal with any questions that come up."

"Can you afford to do that? I know you often sleep at the training facility."

The schedule during the season was insane. He was in meetings all day, every day. He talked to his defensive coordinator, his offensive coordinator, and addressed player concerns. And through it all, he watched film endlessly, studying other teams' plays and tailoring his game plan to best counter each week's opponent. Yet he couldn't regret that time, since it was finally going to pay off this year in the recognition he craved, not just for himself but for the people he'd brought up with him. People who had believed in him.

"You are important to me. I will make time."

He'd surprised her, he could tell. For the first time, he was seeing how much he'd let her down in recent years, focused solely on his own goals. His own friend was surprised to hear how valuable she was to him.

"That's kind of you, but I know you're busy." She frowned. "It's no trouble to simply enjoy the comfort of my own home."

He made an exaggerated effort to look around the room.

"Is this place lacking? Hell, Addy. Upgrade my sheets if they're not to your liking."

"I'm sure your sheets are fine." She set aside her plate and made a grab for her water, taking a long swallow.

He watched the narrow column of her throat and wondered how he'd ever look at her in a purely friendly way again. Just thinking about her under his sheets was enough to spike the temperature in the room. To distract himself from thoughts of her wrapped in Egyptian cotton, he stood, stalking around the table to sit on the otto-man right in front of her, turning his back on the game.

"But?" he prompted, an edge in his voice from the pent-up frustration of this day with her.

"But no matter how lovely your home is, I'd rather be close to my own things. I don't see the benefit of being here."

"The benefit is the complete privacy as well as safety, since the family compound is absolutely secure. No media gets through the front gate." He knew she valued privacy as much as he did. This angle would be more effective than telling her the truth—that he wanted her close at all times so that he would never miss an op-portunity to push his agenda over the next four weeks. "You know as well as I do that public interest in our en-gagement will be high, especially after how thoroughly the press covered my split with Valentina."

"So I hide out here because of a manipulative ex-lover?" Her expression went stony. "I have business to conduct."

"Use my office," he offered, hitting the button to mute the sound on the television. "The facilities are excellent."

She frowned. "I do not like being put in this posi-tion."

He hoped that meant she was done arguing. He couldn't remember ever arguing with Adelaide before today—or at least not since she'd worked for him. "I don't like you leaving, but I'm trying to find a work-able solution."

She opened her mouth to speak and then closed it again.

"What?" he prodded her, wanting to know what was going on in her head.

"I'm not looking forward to being in the public spotlight with you."

"You've been there a million times." He knew because he usually met her gaze a few times during his press conferences, her hazel eyes wordlessly communicating to him if he was staying on track or not.

"Not in a romantic way." She shook her head, a few tendrils of dark hair sliding loose from the haphazard knot she'd created. "We've got the Brighter NOLA fund-raiser coming up, and no matter what you say about how convincing I'll be as your fiancée, I definitely don't look the part."

"Because of all the hair tossing and slinky gowns." That comment of hers still burned. He didn't care for that view of himself. "I believe we've covered that. And if you're correct that I've become too predictable in my dating choices, I'm glad for the chance to shake up public perceptions."

"I didn't mean to suggest you only dated women for their looks." She bit her lip. "The sad truth of the matter is a far more practical concern. I have the wardrobe of an assistant. Not a fiancée."

He tried to hide his grin and failed. "So you're saying we actually need the slinky gowns to pull this off?"

"You don't have to look so damn smug about it," she fired back, making him realize how much he'd missed their friendship.

He held up both hands to show his surrender. "No smugness intended. But I sure don't have time to dress shop this week, Addy, what with our first opponent being the defending National Conference champions and all."

"Wiseass," she chided, shaking her head so that the pencil holding the knot in her hair slipped. She reached up to grab it as the dark mass fell around her shoulders.

He'd seen that move before in private moments with her. Never had it made his mouth water. Or kicked his lust into a full-throttle roar.

Some of what he was feeling must have shown on his face because the hint of a smile she'd been wearing suddenly fled. Pupils dilating, she stood up fast, letting go of her hair and setting aside the pencil.

"I'll figure something out." She stared down at him, her face bathed in the blue glow from the television playing silently in the background, her delicate curves visible through the thin fabric of his too-big T-shirt. "With the wardrobe and with my business. I'll use your office and stay here. It's just for four weeks anyway."

She'd just conceded to everything he'd been angling for, but the reminder of the four-week time limit on their arrangement sure stole any sense of victory he might have felt. Slowly, he got to his feet before she bolted.

"Thank you." He wanted to seal the deal with a handshake. A kiss. A night in his bed. But putting his hands on her now might shatter the tenuous agreement they'd come to in the past few hours.

She deserved so much better from him.

She nodded, the big T-shirt slipping off one shoulder to reveal her golden skin. "I'm going to let you watch your film now."

Edging back a step, she moved away from him, and it took all his willpower not to haul her back.

"For whatever it's worth—I'm proud to call you my

fiancée. To my family, the media. The whole damn world." He thought she deserved to know that much. Today had shown him that he'd taken her friendship for granted too often.

He hadn't paid attention to her—really paid attention—in far too long.

He paid attention now, though. Enough to see the mix of emotions he couldn't read cross her face in quick succession.

"Good night," she said softly, her cheeks pink with confusion.

Watching her retreat, Dempsey turned on the television even as he knew the game film wasn't going to come close to holding his attention the way Adelaide did.

Four

"Sweetheart, stop fidgeting," Adelaide's mother rebuked her, a mouthful of pins muffling the words.

"I'm just nervous." Adelaide stood on a worn vinyl hassock in the one-bedroom apartment on St. Roch Avenue where she'd grown up.

With less than an hour before her first official public appearance with Dempsey, she had realized the gown she'd chosen for the Brighter NOLA foundation fundraiser was too long despite her four-and-a-half-inch heels. She could have phoned the exclusive shop where Dempsey had given her carte blanche, but the price tag had nearly given her heart failure the first time around. She couldn't bring herself to request an emergency tailor visit simply because she'd forgotten her shoes the day she'd chosen the dress.

So instead, she brought the pink lace designer confection to her mother's apartment for a last-minute fix. And perhaps she also craved seeing her mom when she was incredibly nervous. She hadn't been home since her "engagement" had become front-page news in the New Orleans paper and she hated that she couldn't confide the truth to her mother. But she could at least soak up some of her mom's love while she got the hem adjusted—with Evan waiting for her out front in the Land Rover.

"Addy." Her mother straightened, tugging the pins out of her mouth and setting them in the upside-down top of the plastic candy dish on the coffee table. "You're engaged to one of the richest, most powerful men in the state. You could have a dozen seamstresses fixing this gorgeous dress instead of your half-blind mama. You know better than to trust a woman who needs bifocals to do this job."

Guilt pinched Adelaide more than her silver-and-pink stilettos.

"You're not half-blind," she argued, leaning down to kiss her mother's cheek and breathing in the scent of lemon verbena. "And you could sew stitches around anyone working on Magazine Street. But I'm sorry to foist off the job on you last minute. I just missed you and I didn't want a snippy tailor frowning at my choice of shoes or thinking how my breasts don't suit the elegant lines of the gown."

Her mother gave her a narrow look. Taller than Adelaide, her mother was a commanding woman who had worked hard to raise Adelaide after her father died in a boating accident when she was just a toddler. Della Thibodeaux had given Adelaide her backbone, but there were days when Addy wished she'd gotten more of that particular trait. Her creativity and her dreamy nature were qualities she'd inherited from her father, apparently. But it was her mother's unflinching work ethic that had helped Adelaide excel at being Dempsey's assistant.

"Bite your tongue," Della said. "How will you survive your future mother-in-law if you can't put an uppity dress-shop girl in her place?"

"I know. I'm being ridiculous." She blinked fast, trying to control her emotions. It had been a crazy week fulfilling her duties as Dempsey's assistant while maintaining her commitments to her new business. And now she had a role to play as his fiancée, all the while fighting off waves of nostalgia for what she'd felt for him in the past. "Living the Reynaud life with Dempsey has put my emotions on a roller-coaster ride. I'm not used to the way the Reynauds can just…order the world to their liking."

From personal chefs to chauffeurs, there was no service that wasn't available to Dempsey around the clock. And now to her, too. While she'd witnessed that degree of luxury from a business standpoint for years, she hadn't really appreciated the way there were no limits in his personal life. He'd offered to have designers send samples from Paris for tonight's gown, for crying out loud.

And the ring he'd ordered for her… She'd nearly fainted when she'd opened the package hand delivered by a courier who'd arrived at the house with a security escort earlier in the day. The massive yellow diamond surrounded by smaller white ones had literally taken her breath away.

Between the ring—temporarily stashed in her purse,

since it seemed over-the-top for her mother's house—and the dress, she'd started to understand how closely scrutinized she would be as Dempsey's fiancée. It increased the pressure for tonight tenfold.

"My sweet girl." Her mom spared a moment to put a hand to Adelaide's cheek. "If you *are* emotional, is there any chance you could be pregnant?"

"Mom!" Embarrassed, she fluffed the hem to see how the length was coming. "There is no chance of that."

Her mom studied her for an extra second before bending to her task again. Della took up the needle and continued to make long stitches to anchor the hemline.

"Well, you must admit the engagement came a bit out of the blue. People are bound to talk." Her mother straightened, still wearing purple scrubs from her shift at the hospital where she'd worked for as long as Adelaide could remember.

She hadn't thought about that. "Well, it's not true, and the world will know soon enough when I don't start showing. I just want tonight to go well." She kicked out the sagging hem of her gorgeous dress. "I feel as if I'm off to a bad start already since I lost time to do my makeup and my hair when I realized I had a wardrobe malfunction."

Her mother frowned. "Addy, you just got engaged. You should be glowing with joy, not running to your mother and fretting about your makeup. Are you going to tell me what's wrong?"

Closing her eyes, she realized her mistake in coming here. Her mother didn't suffer fools lightly. And Adelaide was taking the most foolish risk of her life to put herself in close proximity to Dempsey every day and night. What if her old crush on him returned?

Actually…what if it already had? Remembering the

way her thoughts short-circuited whenever they had spent time alone together this week, she had to wonder.

"You know I've always liked Dempsey," she began, unwilling to lie to her mother.

She could at least confide a little piece of her heart to the woman who knew her best.

"I would have to have been blind not to see the adoration in your face from the time you were a girl." Her mother went back to sewing, taking a seat on the chair next to the hassock. "Yes, honey. I recall you've always liked him."

"Well, his proposal caught me by surprise," she admitted, her gaze rising over the sofa and settling on the wooden shelves containing her mother's treasures— photos of Adelaide, mostly. "And I want to be sure—" she cleared her throat "—that he asked me to marry him for the right reasons. I don't want to just be convenient."

Her mother paused and then resumed her sewing. Adelaide waited for her mom's verdict, all the while focusing on a chipped pink teacup Adelaide had painted for her for Mother's Day in grade school.

"Damn straight you don't," her mother said finally. "That boy's whole life has been *convenient* ever since he was whisked out of town in a limo." She knotted the thread once. Twice. And snapped it off. "Maybe you should ruffle his feathers a little? Catch *him* by surprise."

"You think so?" Adelaide worried her lip, remembering she'd better start her makeup if she didn't want to be late.

Evan had made her promise she'd be finished in time to meet Dempsey outside the event promptly at 7:00 p.m. so they could walk in together. A shiver of nerves—and undeniable excitement—raced up her spine.

"Honey, I know so." Her mother held out a hand to help Adelaide down to the floor. "You've made yourself very available to that man—"

"He's my boss," she reminded her.

"Even so." She shook her finger in Adelaide's face. "He's not going to be the boss in the marriage, is he? No. Marriage should be a partnership. So don't let him think you're going to be the same woman as a bride that you are as his assistant."

Easy enough advice if her engagement were real. But for the next few weeks, she was still more an employee than a fiancée. Then again, he had looked at her with decided heat in his eyes ever since that accidental touch in the stadium last weekend. And truth be told, it stung that he thought he could boss her into an engagement when they were supposed to be friends.

"Maybe I will surprise him." She picked up her makeup and went to work on her eyes, hoping to look more like an exotic beauty and less like an efficient, capable assistant.

Mascara helped. Besides, she'd gone to art school. If she couldn't create a good smoky eye, she ought to turn in her degree.

"No maybe about it." Her mother went to work on Adelaide's hair, her fingers brushing through the long caramel-colored strands. "This dress is a good start." She winked at Adelaide's reflection in the hallway mirror. "You don't look like anyone's assistant tonight."

"How close are you?" Dempsey shifted the phone against his ear as his hired driver pulled up to the venue in Jackson Square.

He'd left the Land Rover and Evan with Adelaide

this week, trusting his regular driver to keep her safe. By safe, Dempsey had meant keeping reporters away. He'd never imagined his temporary fiancée would have a sudden desire to visit the old neighborhood.

A tic started behind his eye as he thought about her there without him. She'd moved to an apartment closer to the French Quarter after college, but her mom had never left the place on St. Roch. Even Dempsey's mother had found greener pastures nearer the lake.

But then, his mother had the financial cushion of whatever his father had paid her to keep clear of Dempsey.

"Two minutes, max," Evan assured him. "I'm right behind the building, just crawling with the traffic."

"I'll walk toward you." Dempsey exited the vehicle close to Muriel's, the historic restaurant chosen for the event. Then he sent the driver on his way.

He would have preferred to pick up Adelaide personally tonight, but practice had run long and the meetings afterward had been longer still. There was unrest among some of the younger guys on the offensive line, but Dempsey was leaving the peacekeeping to his brother Henri, their starting quarterback. Henri had mastered the art of letting things roll off him, which was key for a player who operated under a microscope every week.

But the same quality could tick off other guys in the locker room, the players who took every setback like a personal affront, the athletes who were competitive to the point of obsessive. The media loved to key in on crap like that.

And with the press hinting at marital trouble in Henri's private life, the team's front man wasn't exactly feeling friendly toward the local sports journalists.

Dempsey just hoped he would get through the fundraiser tonight. No matter what was going on in Henri's personal world, he trusted the guy to lead them to a win Sunday.

"I see you." Evan's voice in his ear brought him back to the present, where he damn well needed to stay. "I'm going to pull right up to the curb for the sake of Miss Adelaide's shoes."

Looking up the street, Dempsey spied the Land Rover headed his way. He pocketed the phone and moved toward the red carpet that had been laid on the sidewalk. Players were already arriving along with prominent local politicians, artists and philanthropists. A lone trumpeter in a white suit serenaded the guests on their way into the Jackson Square landmark venue.

A staffer from the Brighter NOLA foundation hurried toward Dempsey to pin a flower to his jacket and update him on the guest list so far. He thanked her and waved the woman off as the Land Rover arrived in front of the carpet.

He didn't care about protocol, so he didn't wait for Evan to open Adelaide's door. Dempsey tugged open the handle himself and extended a hand to…

Wow.

All thoughts of guests, players and philanthropy vanished at the sight of Adelaide. She wore a pink dress that might possibly be described as "lace," but it was a far cry from a granny's doily. Beaded and shimmering, the gown hugged her curves all over. It wasn't low cut. It was long-sleeved and it fell to her toes. Yet the lace effect made strategic portions of her honey-toned skin visible right through the rosy-toned mesh. Her thighs, for example. The indentations above her hips.

Intellectually, he'd always known she was an attractive woman. Of course he had. He wasn't blind. But maybe her workday wardrobe had helped minimize an appeal that damn near staggered him now. With an effort, he dragged his attention away from her body to meet her gaze.

Only to find a simmering heat there that matched his own.

This engagement charade of his was feeling far too real. And if he wasn't careful, he would end up following that heat where it led and hurting Adelaide in the process. That was the last thing he wanted.

The very last thing he could afford.

"You look beautiful." He tugged her closer, wrapping an arm around her waist to escort her inside.

She smelled fantastic. Like night-blooming roses. Her hair was gathered at the back of her head, some of it coiled and braided, with strands left loose to curl around her face. She wore her waist-length hair up most days, wound into a simple knot. The soft curls trailing to the middle of her back made him wonder when was the last time he'd seen her with her hair let down.

"Thank you." She kept a tight hold on a beaded pink purse, the engagement ring he'd produced for her glinting on her left hand. "And thank you for the ring," she added softly, for his ears only as they walked toward the entrance behind slow-moving attendees meeting and greeting one another. "I've never seen anything so gorgeous."

He'd ordered it immediately after announcing the engagement to ensure the custom design would be crafted in time for tonight's party. He hated that he'd had to have it shipped to her at the house instead of giving it to her in person, however.

Then again, with their roles feeling a little too real, it was probably for the best he hadn't personally slipped that big yellow diamond onto her finger.

"Adelaide!" someone on the street called out to her, and she halted. Turned.

A camera flash popped nearby as a woman snapped a photo of them.

"Are you aware that Valentina Rushnaya will be attending tonight's event?" the photographer shouted over the trumpet music and din of nearby conversation.

Dempsey tensed, ready to respond. Addy beat him to it.

"How kind of her to support a Brighter NOLA future." Adelaide smiled as she lifted a hand to his chest and tipped her head to his shoulder as if they were a couple in love.

Was she simply posing for another photo? Or showing off the ring?

He followed her lead, kissing the top of her head possessively before ushering her toward the door.

"Nicely done." He wished he could pull her into a dark corner and talk to her. Make sure she was solid going into this event if Valentina truly put in an appearance. But there was no time now as people were already headed their way. "Let's stick together for the first half hour."

"Of course." She smiled her public smile, already waving to one of their biggest donors. "But you're dancing with me tonight," she warned him. "It's the perk of being your fiancée."

Normally, Dempsey worked the floor of a fund-raiser

with precision, glad-handing the necessary parties and then leaving, never giving in to Adelaide's invitations to stay longer and have fun. But this was his foundation and he was here for the long haul.

"The perk is all mine." The words fell out of his mouth before they were surrounded by well-wishers, potential patrons and community bigwigs.

Dempsey noticed Adelaide went into work mode as quickly as he did, but his focus was nowhere near his usual level. Even as he made conversation, his thoughts went back to those moments on the red carpet with Adelaide. The way she'd looked when she stepped from the Land Rover and every soul in Jackson Square had let out a collective breath. The way she'd curled against him when that photographer wanted a picture, as though she'd been born to be in his arms.

The idea bothered him.

There was no doubt in his mind that Adelaide looked different tonight, from how she wore her hair to that dress of hers that was killing him. And as the night wore on, he couldn't take his eyes off her. He wondered who she was talking to and if they noticed that she looked like a walking fantasy. Part of him wanted confirmation that something about her had changed, but another part of him wanted to make sure every other man in the building wasn't looking at her, because he didn't want anyone else thinking about her thighs.

Maybe he really had been blind all those years they'd just been friends.

Two hours into the event, the night seemed to be running smoothly enough. Casino tables had opened around the rooms blocked off for the party. The red walls and decadent furnishings of Muriel's legendary

Séance Lounge made an appealing backdrop for black-jack as the crowd loosened up. The gaming was strictly to raise money for Brighter NOLA. It was so packed that guests stood out on the balconies in the heat, snapping photos of themselves with Jackson Square in the background. The dance floor was filled and the band—as always in this town—sounded fantastic.

He was about to seek out Adelaide when a feminine voice purred in his right ear.

"My lone wolf looks on edge tonight." The low tone and soft consonants of Valentina's Russian accent made him tense.

Turning, he avoided her attempt to kiss his cheek.

"If I'm on edge, it's only because you've taken up the valuable time of my staff with empty threats and games." He gave her a level look, noting that her barely there silver gown was completely over-the-top for a charity event that raised funds for underprivileged and at-risk youths.

"Your staff? Or your fiancée?" She tossed her head in a dismissive gesture meant to be insulting.

Dempsey had to smother a mirthless laugh because—damn it to hell—Adelaide had been correct about him dating theatrical women in slinky gowns. When had he become such a cliché?

"Both." He was grateful they stood in the shadows, since he didn't need photos of them together showing up in the paper. "And I trust the only reason you're here is to write a big, fat check to the foundation, since we specifically agreed to go our separate ways."

"Agreed? There was no agreement!" She pulled a glass of champagne off a passing waiter's tray and helped herself to a long sip. "You dictated every detail of our time together, and then disappeared before my bed even had time to cool down—"

"Ms. Rushnaya, how beautiful you look." Adelaide appeared at his side, slipping an arm through his. "I'm so sorry to interrupt, but, Dempsey, we did promise a quick word with the representative from *Town and Country* before they leave."

She nodded meaningfully toward the other side of the room.

"Of course." He had always counted on Addy for well-timed interruptions, and she delivered yet again. Still, he didn't like that she'd overheard the bit about running out of Valentina's bed. He didn't treat women that way. "Please excuse us."

"Yes, do take your turn with *Town and Country*." Valentina emptied her glass and set it on a nearby table, her movements unsteady. "I have my own press to speak with, Dempsey."

She turned on her heel to march away, right toward a woman who had a camera aimed at them. Again.

"Dempsey." Adelaide laid her hand on his cheek and turned his face toward her, commanding his attention before the camera flashed. "There isn't actually an interview," she confided. "I was just trying to give you some breathing room."

The look in her hazel eyes stole all his focus. Or maybe it was the gentle press of her breasts as she arched closer.

"Thank you." How many times had she served as a buffer for him with the media or with football insiders he didn't particularly like? She ran interference like a pro.

"Dance with me?" she asked, a hint of uncertainty in her gaze.

Had he put that vulnerability there? He hadn't spent much time with her this evening, handling the room with the same "divide and conquer" approach they'd used in the past at events he'd needed to attend. But tonight was different. Or at least, it should be. If he'd had Adelaide by his side earlier, Valentina might not have tried to ambush him in a dark corner.

"With pleasure." He lifted Adelaide's hand to his mouth and brushed a kiss along her knuckles. Her skin smelled like roses.

He'd done it to reassure her that he wanted to be with her. To thank her for sending Valentina on her way.

At least, the kiss started out with good intentions. But as the slow blues tune hit a long, sultry note, Dempsey couldn't seem to let her go. Adelaide was getting under his skin tonight, and it wasn't just that damnable dress. So he flipped her hand over and placed a kiss in her palm, where he felt her pulse flutter under his lips. Which made him think about all the other ways he could send her heart racing. All the pulse points he could cover with his mouth. In turn, his own heart slugged harder inside his chest.

Every damn thing got harder.

"My song will be over by the time we get out there," she whispered, though she didn't sound terribly disappointed.

Her pupils dilated so wide there was just a hint of color around the edges.

"It's less crowded right here." He wanted her to himself, he realized. Craved her, in fact. "Plenty of room to dance."

"Really?" She peered around them. "I guess it's the kind of thing an engaged couple would do."

"Exactly." He pulled her into his arms, fitting her curves against him, close enough to catch her scent, but not nearly as close as he'd like. "No sense letting anyone think Valentina caused any drama."

At the mention of the woman's name, Addy's gaze dropped. He cursed himself for being an idiot as he backed them closer to the open doors leading out to the balcony.

"Is that what this whole charade is about?" she asked when she looked up at him again. "Have I been promoted to your round-the-clock protection from the she-wolves of the world?"

She couldn't be jealous. Yet the thought nearly made him miss a step.

"No." He lowered his voice, knowing how the walls had ears at events like this. "You and I have a whole lot more at stake between us and I think you know it."

"If there's more at stake, you might want to up your game while we're in public, since newly engaged men don't tend to prowl the perimeters of parties alone." She practically vibrated in his arms as he drew her out onto the balcony and into the farthest deserted corner.

He couldn't remember the last time she'd spoken to him with so much fire in her eyes.

"You're jealous." He tested the idea by saying it out loud as he studied her in the moonlight. The song came to an end.

He didn't let go of her.

"And you're *mine* for four weeks, Dempsey Reynaud." She tipped her chin up at him. "I suggest you act like it if you want to pull off this ruse of your own making."

Heat rushed up his spine in a molten blast. The need to offer her what she'd asked for made him grip her tighter, pulling her hip to hip, chest to breasts.

And if that was a little too much PDA for a charity event, too damn bad. It wasn't anywhere near enough for what he wanted to do with her. She felt even better up close than he'd imagined, and his head had been full of inventive scenarios all week.

"Careful what you wish for, Addy," he warned her, grateful for the night shadows that kept them hidden.

He'd been a gentleman for her sake. At least now she would know exactly how much he was feeling like her fiancé. Her hips cradled the hard length he couldn't begin to hide.

And that was when things got crazy. Because instead of storming off like his affronted best friend, Adelaide gripped the lapels of his tuxedo and pressed a kiss to his lips.

Five

Adelaide saw stars.

Clutching Dempsey's jacket, she fulfilled a secret dream as her lips brushed along his. They stood under the night sky, his back shielding her from view. Behind her, the iron bars of the balcony pressed against her spine. In front of her, warm male muscle was equally unyielding but oh-so-enticing.

She'd seen a chance to surprise him—just as her mother had suggested—and she'd taken it. She knew better than to think this fake engagement was going anywhere. But she could use this time to indulge herself and her long-standing fantasies about Dempsey. Because in less than four weeks, things were going to change between them forever when she left her job with the Hurricanes.

Her senses reeling, she broke the kiss, needing to

put some distance between them. He didn't move far from her, though. It took another long moment before he released her.

"Let's go," he urged, threading his fingers through hers and claiming a hand.

Blinking through the fog of desire, Adelaide followed him, her steps smaller and quicker by necessity due to the fitted gown. Her lips tingled pleasantly, her nerve endings humming with awareness of the man beside her.

"Are you sure we should leave?" She glanced around the private rooms at the full dance floor, the crammed gaming tables, the busy bar stations. "As hosts of the event—"

"We've done our part," he assured her. "The event planner will take it from here. And I'm dying to get you alone."

To explore what she'd started? She hadn't missed the indication of attraction when she'd been pressed up against him. But she couldn't afford to trade her heart for a night in his bed, and she knew herself well enough to know that was a very real possibility. Her feelings for Dempsey had always been strong. Complicated. And this engagement wasn't exactly simplifying matters.

"I didn't mean to send mixed signals." She hated to have this conversation here, in a quiet corridor as they waited for an elevator. But it was too important to wait. "I got caught up in the moment—" She bit her lip to refrain from telling him about her mother's suggestion that she surprise him.

She'd taken the gamble, but she wasn't sure she was ready for the payout he had in mind.

"Will you promise me something?" His eyes searched

hers, as if he could see straight through to her heart. "Will you think about how rewarding it could be to get caught up in another moment? Not tonight, maybe. But we've got a lot of days to spend together and I think there's something worth exploring in that kiss."

Her heart did a little flip that made her feel woozy and breathless at the same time. She settled for a nod, unable to articulate an answer just now.

He pressed a button for the elevator and stepped into the cabin behind her when it arrived. His grandfather, family patriarch Leon Reynaud, stood against one wall inside the elevator. Adelaide didn't know him well, but he attended all of the Hurricanes home games and she'd seen him in the owner's suite on the fifty-yard line a few times.

He'd been a big man in another era, playing football and becoming a successful team owner of a Texas franchise until he'd sold it to be closer to his grandsons in Louisiana. But the years had bowed his back and he'd grown much thinner. Dempsey had told her once that Leon had never considered himself a good parent to his own sons and because of that, he tried harder to be a presence for his grandsons. Adelaide knew for a fact the older man held far more of Dempsey's respect than his philandering father, Theo.

"Hello, Mr. Reynaud," she greeted him while Dempsey clapped him on the shoulder.

"We're heading home, Grand-père. Do you need a ride?" Dempsey asked.

"No need. I want to try my hand at blackjack and see if the Reynaud luck holds." He gave Adelaide a rakish grin and straightened his already perfect tie. "My dear, did you know my own grandfather won his first boat in a game of cards? From there, he grew the Zephyr Shipping empire."

It was a much-loved bit of Reynaud lore.

"Adelaide probably knows the family history as well as I do." Dempsey met her gaze for a moment and she drank in the compliment.

He rarely handed out praise, especially publicly. The elevator bell chimed, and the door opened to the first floor. She stepped out into the crowd while Dempsey held the door for his grandfather.

"Adelaide, you say?" Leon frowned as he moved slowly toward the bar, his expression blank for a moment before his gray brows furrowed. "Be careful with the ladies, son. You wouldn't want your wife to find out."

"But, Grand-père—" Dempsey called after him as the older man disappeared into the crowd. Turning toward her, Dempsey pulled out his phone. "He's been getting more confused lately."

"Should we stay with him?" Adelaide hadn't heard about Leon having any moments of confusion, but then, Dempsey didn't share much about his family outside of business concerns.

Some of the magic of their kiss evaporated with the reminder of how removed she was from his private life. Even as his so-called fiancée.

"I'm texting Evan. He has a friend here tonight providing extra security. I'll have him keep an eye on Leon and make sure he gets home safely."

"One of your brothers might still be here." She peered back into the party. "I saw Henri with some of the other players—"

"It's handled." He tucked his phone in his pocket and pressed a hand to her lower back.

A perfunctory touch. A social nicety. She could feel that his attention had drifted from her. From them.

Ha. Who was she kidding? There was no *them*. Dempsey maneuvered her now the same way he orchestrated the rest of his world. He wasn't the kind of man to be carried away by a kiss, and right now he clearly had other things on his mind.

Forcing her thoughts from the chemistry that had simmered between them, Adelaide promised herself not to act on any more impulsive longings. She'd wanted to shake things up a bit between them and she had. But his silence on the ride home told her all she needed to know about the gamble she'd taken with the kiss.

It hadn't paid off.

From now on, she would take her cues from Dempsey. If he wanted their relationship to be focused on business, she only had three and a half more weeks to pretend that old crush of hers hadn't fired to life all over again.

The next day, she balanced two coffees in a tray and a box of pastries from Dempsey's favorite bakery as she strode through the training facility toward his office. She reminded herself she'd done the same thing for him plenty of other times in her years as his assistant. When they'd been in Atlanta together and Dempsey had still been an assistant coach, they'd shared a secret addiction to apple fritters and she'd grown skilled at sneaking them into the training complex so the health-minded nutritionists wouldn't discover them.

Now that they were back in New Orleans, Adelaide knew to pick up beignets on game days when they were downtown. But in Metairie, for an occasional treat, she bought raspberry scones. Technically, procuring pastries wasn't on her formal list of duties. And maybe it was her sweet tooth that had driven this one shared pleasure. But after last night's awkward end to the evening, she found herself wanting to put their relationship back on familiar ground.

It wasn't as if she was offended that her kiss hadn't made him realize he'd always loved her from afar or had some other fairy-tale outcome. But maybe she'd dreamed once or twice that such a thing could really happen if they ever kissed. That Dempsey would see her with new eyes and forget about the Valentinas of the world.

Right. He'd made it clear she would be welcome in his bed, but he hadn't seemed inclined to consider what that would mean for them—their friendship, their work together or even this farce of an engagement. How could she knowingly walk into an intimate relationship with him when she'd seen the devastation he left in his wake?

The sun hadn't even risen that morning when she'd awoken to an empty house, and she'd known that Dempsey had left for work. He'd been restless when they'd arrived home after the charity fund-raiser, excusing himself to call his brother Jean-Pierre in New York. She'd thought then that maybe he was more upset about his grandfather's mistake than he'd let on. Why else would he call Jean-Pierre when it would have been after midnight in Manhattan?

Unless he'd been fighting the riot of yearning that had plagued her.

She backed into the double doors leading to the front

offices and nearly ran into Pat Tyrell, the Hurricanes' defensive coordinator.

"Well, good morning, Miss Adelaide." He tipped his team hat to her since, even at seventy years old, the grizzled old coach was still a flirt. "Those wouldn't happen to be illicit treats in that white pastry box of yours?"

The older man knew her well. He held the door open for her.

"I figured I didn't have to hide them at this hour since the trainers won't be in until at least nine o'clock." She lifted the box toward him. "Want a raspberry scone?"

"You speak an old man's language." His black-and-gold windbreaker crinkled as he reached into the box to help himself. "Dempsey ought to be ready for breakfast soon. I came in this morning to find him running up and down the bleachers like a kid in training camp."

Her mouth went dry as she envisioned Dempsey in his workout routine. He was as fit as any of his players, even if she did manage to tempt him into an occasional scone.

"Maybe he's getting ready to run a few plays himself on Sunday." She sidestepped Pat to head into her office. "He's always saying we need more discipline on the field."

"Damn shame that boy didn't have a shot to play in the NFL. When you get that kind of football mind combined with talent, it's a beautiful thing to watch." He raised his pastry in salute. "Thanks for the sweets, Addy."

Settling into her small office next door to Dempsey's massive suite, Adelaide set down the coffees and dropped her purse on the floor beside the desk. She'd only been joking about Dempsey getting ready to run plays. Maybe because she wasn't a football player she hadn't given much thought to the fact that Dempsey's decorated college career as a tight end had never gone to the next level. He'd told her once that he'd chosen to coach because he could bring more to the game that way, and she believed him.

But she also knew from articles in the media that an injury in his youth had never mended properly and that another hit to his spine could paralyze him—something that his college coaches hadn't known about, but had been quickly discovered in a physical by the team that had drafted him. Dempsey had been on a plane back to Louisiana the next day and, Adelaide recalled, Leon Reynaud had threatened to sue the college where he'd played.

At the time, she'd been busy finishing up her fine arts degree and debating whether to apply to a master's program. She'd also been in recovery mode from her crush on Dempsey and had been trying to ignore the stories about him.

The knock on her office door startled her from her thoughts. Dempsey appeared in the doorway in cargo shorts and a black team polo shirt that fit him to perfection. His hair, still wet from the shower, was even darker than usual. He hadn't shaved either. The jaw that had been well groomed just twelve hours ago for the charity ball was already heavily shadowed.

"Morning." He strode past her desk to stand by the window overlooking the training field, where a few players were loosening up even though official warm-ups wouldn't start for another hour or more. "I didn't expect you today."

She'd worked overtime this week, as she did most

weeks. But he seemed to understand her desire to devote some hours to her own business because he'd told her last night that she should take the day off.

She watched him now, struck anew by his masculine appeal. After all the years she'd known him, she would have hoped to have been used to him. Some days, when they were embroiled in work, she managed to forget that he was an incredibly magnetic male. Other times, the raw virility of him made her a little light-headed, like now.

"You seemed so distracted last night, I wasn't even sure you would remember saying that." She handed him his coffee and joined him at the window. She tracked the movements of two new receivers racing each other down the field.

Every day she encountered virile, handsome men. Men that other women swooned over on game days. What was it about Dempsey alone that drew her eye?

"I meant it." He sipped his coffee and stared at her until her skin grew warm with awareness. "I'm worried about Leon."

That shifted her focus in a hurry. She couldn't remember the last time he'd shared a personal concern with her.

"He thought he was speaking to Theo last night when he told you to be careful your wife didn't find out about me." She knew that Theo Reynaud had a notorious reputation, dating back to his years as a college athlete and straight through his time as a pro.

His wife had left him shortly after Dempsey—the son of an extramarital affair—arrived in her household. She'd told Dempsey that he was her "last straw."

"Right." He shook his head. "We've known that he

has episodes of confusion, but he claimed he saw a doctor who diagnosed it as a thyroid problem. I looked it up, because I wasn't sure if we could believe him, but that is a possibility."

"So either he's not taking the right medicines for it—"

"Or he's been BSing us the whole time and he's never seen a doctor. He's as hardheaded as they come and he doesn't put much faith in the health-care system."

"He is always telling the trainers not to coddle the players." She'd heard him bark at the medical staff often enough, imparting a "tough it out" mentality.

"Exactly." Dempsey frowned. "I asked Jean-Pierre to try to spend some time down here this season so we can present a united front to get Leon evaluated and, if necessary, into more aggressive medical treatment."

Reaching toward her desk, she pulled the box of scones closer.

"Jean-Pierre will have to come home for Gervais's wedding." She'd tracked the wedding talk on social media as part of her duties managing Dempsey's profile pages online. With the Hurricanes' owner marrying a foreign princess, the topic had more traction than any other team news.

The fact that there'd been no official announcement only fueled the rumor mill until speculating on the whens and hows of the nuptials filled page after page of gossip blogs.

"That's still six weeks away." He relinquished his coffee to grab a couple of paper plates from her stash near the minifridge. "I think we need to act soon. I don't want something to happen to Leon because we're all too damn busy to pay attention to the warning signs.

We owe him better, even though he's not going to be happy about us strong-arming him."

"Will you invite your dad to be there?" She took a plate and a scone and passed him the box. "Or any of the rest of the family?"

Leon had another son who lived in Texas, and one out on the West Coast, and there were cousins as well, but the relationships had been strained for a long time.

"No. If Theo happens to be in town, fine." His jaw flexed at the mention of his father, a tic shared by all of Theo's sons. "But I'm not going to seek him out for a family event that will be stressful enough as it is." He set aside his breakfast.

Then slipped hers from her hands and set it on the desk.

"Is that a hint?" she asked, her gaze following the bit of raspberry heaven now out of reach. "Am I indulging my sweet tooth too often?"

"Of course not. I wanted to apologize for last night." He took her hand between his and gave her his undivided attention.

Making her whole body go on full alert.

"You don't owe me any apologies." She hadn't expected a discussion about what happened and, consequently, was completely unprepared.

"I do. I didn't pick you up last night to bring you to the event. I didn't deliver your engagement ring personally. And then the episode with my grandfather distracted me from one of the most shockingly provocative kisses of my life."

"Oh." Completely. Unprepared. "I—"

"Can I ask you a personal question?"

Her heart hammered so loudly in her ears she wasn't

entirely sure she'd hear it, but she nodded. The warmth of his palm on the back of her hand sent sparks of pleasure pinging around her insides.

"Have you thought about us that way before? Or is this a whole new experience, feeling all that chemistry?" His golden-brown gaze captured hers.

Her cheeks heated and she cursed the reaction bitterly even as she shrugged like an inarticulate teenager. But answering the question felt like a "damned if she did, damned if she didn't" proposition.

"Right." He let go of her hand. "Maybe I have no business asking you that. But I'll admit I'm having a tough time concentrating today. I came in early just to hit the gym and try to work off some steam because I damn well couldn't sleep."

That got her attention.

"Because of me?" Her voice sounded as though she'd been sucking down helium. She grabbed her coffee and took a healthy swig.

"Things got heated last night, wouldn't you agree?" His voice lowered. Deepened.

The words felt like a stroke along her skin, they were so damn seductive. But she needed to proceed with extreme caution. She'd heard Valentina's accusation the night before. Dempsey had left her bed before the sheets cooled, according to her.

"That's what happens when you play games and pretend things you don't feel." She kept her cool, needing to make herself heard before she did something foolish, like respond to all that simmering heat she felt when he touched her. "You can't tell where the game ends and reality begins."

For one heart-stopping moment, she imagined what

would happen if he kissed her this time. If he laid her on her desk and told her the games ended here and now. She could almost taste the moment, it felt so real.

"Why does it have to be a game?" He edged back from her, his gaze level. "We've always been good together. We respect each other. Why not enjoy the benefits of this attraction now that it's becoming a distraction?"

She could hear the influence of his Reynaud roots in his word choices. It took a superhuman effort not to roll her eyes.

"Maybe because I don't think of relationships in terms of benefits. We're talking about intimacy, not some contractual arrangement. And I definitely don't want to be pursued for the sake of a distraction."

"I wouldn't be so quick to write off the advantages." He took a step closer. Crowding her. "Perhaps we should make a list of all the ways you would directly benefit."

Her heart galloped. Her skin seemed to shrink, creating the sensation of being too tight to fit. She didn't think she'd make it through a discussion of the ways having Dempsey in her bed would reward her.

"Maybe some other time." She tossed her empty coffee cup in the trash and stood. "Now that I know you were serious about that day off, maybe I'll just head back to the house and do some work on my designs." She would preserve some dignity, damn it.

Although she did take the box of scones.

The light in his eyes told her that he was on to her. That he understood why she needed to beat a hasty retreat.

"Good. I'm coming home early tonight. I'll take you out for dinner."

Alone?

Her mouth went dry.

"Maybe," she hedged, backing toward the door. "I've got a meeting with a fabric company downtown later. But I'll text you afterward."

She didn't wait for his response as she walked out into the corridor. Her skin hummed with awareness from being around him and from the knowledge that he wanted her. Her kiss—practically a chaste brush of lips—had shifted the dynamic between them more than she'd imagined possible.

Dempsey wanted her.

And maybe, for now, that ought to be enough. She couldn't expect him to fall head over heels for her when he'd hardly seen her as a woman up until earlier in the week. Was she a fool to run away from the firestorm she'd created?

Part of her wanted to march back into her office and strip off all his clothes. Request that detailed list of relationship benefits after all.

Except, of course, she had little experience with men. And baiting a Reynaud was a dangerous business when she wasn't a man-eating Valentina type who could deal with the fallout. She was just Adelaide Thibodeaux and she had a feeling she might never recover from a night in Dempsey's bed. Knowing her overinflated sense of loyalty, she'd probably be lovesick for life, stuck in a job as his assistant in the hope he'd one day crook his finger in her direction so she could repeat the mind-blowing experience.

No, thank you.

Dempsey might have started this game on his terms, but she planned to finish it. On hers.

Six

Dempsey made no claim to being an intuitive man.

But even he could sense that he'd made some headway with Adelaide earlier in the day. Sure, he understood her reluctance to jeopardize their friendship. And he meant what he'd said about respecting her. Caring about her.

Yet the flame that burned between them now wouldn't go away just because they ignored it. She might not be ready to address it, but he sure as hell would. So now he found himself driving around downtown New Orleans in search of the fabric supplier she was using as a pretext for not meeting him for dinner.

He'd rearranged his day and moved his nonnegotiable meetings earlier in the afternoon. His practice had gone well. His game plan for Sunday was solid. Nothing was going to stand in the way of spending time with her tonight. He would make a case for exploring this attraction in a way he hadn't been prepared to do last night after that unsettling talk with Leon.

He needed to get to know her better—a damn sorry thing to admit when he ought to know her as well as anyone. But he'd been too caught up in his own career the past few years to pay attention to Addy. If he wanted to persuade her to let her guard down and give him a chance, he needed to understand what made her happy. What pleased her.

Spotting the storefront of the warehouse, Dempsey steered his BMW sedan into a spot on the street. Evan had driven Adelaide to this location, so Dempsey had it on good authority she was still inside.

The least he could do was show an interest in the business she wanted to start. He'd looked over her business plan briefly before driving out here and he'd been both impressed and worried. Her goals were sound, but fulfilling them would mean a lot of hands-on involvement to get it up and running. Maybe if he discussed the clothing company with her in detail, he'd see a way for her to hand off some of the less important tasks. There had to be a way to free her up enough to keep working with him.

He needed Adelaide.

In the ten steps it took to hit the front door he was already sweating, the heat still wet as a dishcloth even though it was six o'clock. The man seated at the desk out front pointed Dempsey in the right direction, and he went into the warehouse to look for Adelaide.

He found her in front of a display of laces, draping an intricate gray pattern over her calf as if to see what the material looked like up against bare skin. Making him wonder what kinds of garments she had in mind for her next design project.

A vision of her high, full breasts covered in nothing but lace and his hands blasted to the forefront of his brain, making him hotter than the late-afternoon sun had. She wore different clothes from the ones she'd had on at the training facility, trading dark pants and a Hurricanes T-shirt for the yellow-and-blue floral sundress she now wore. Wide-set straps and a square neckline framed her feminine curves. Her hair was rolled into some kind of updo that exposed her neck and made him want to lick it. So much for keeping his thoughts friendly.

"Dempsey?" She straightened, a smile lighting up her face for a moment before a wary look chased after it. "What a surprise to see you here." She gestured to the soaring shelves of fabric samples on miniature hangers, sorted by color and material. "Are you here to redesign the Hurricanes jerseys?"

He scanned a section of striped and polka-dotted cotton.

"I think the guys will stick with what we have." He peered around the warehouse to gauge their level of privacy. He'd seen one other shopper on his way in, but other than that, the space appeared empty. "I'm here for you."

The lace dropped from her fingers. "Is there a problem with our opening day? I checked my phone—"

He caught her hand before she could dig in her purse for the device.

"No problems. Things are running just as they should for the regular-season opener."

He couldn't even touch her anymore without images

of that tentative kiss of hers heating him from the inside out. He didn't know how he'd found the willpower to let her retreat to her own room last night when the need for a better taste of her rode his back like a tackle he couldn't break.

"Then, what did you need?" She slid her hand away from his, making him wonder what she felt when they touched.

"What do I need? To see you." He huffed out a breath and braced an elbow on one of the nearby shelves. "I came here to insist on that dinner I offered since it seemed as though you're being elusive today, and it's bugging me that I don't know why."

She busied herself with returning the lace to its small hanger and finding the proper place to reshelve it. When she didn't respond, he continued, "But now that I'm here, it occurs to me that the bigger reason I needed to see you is that I can't seem to think about anything else."

He watched as her busy movements slowed. Stopped. Color washed her cheeks, confirming his suspicion that she suffered from the same madness as he did. And yes, it gave him tremendous amounts of male satisfaction to think he wasn't the only one feeling it.

She clutched a handful of indigo-colored silk and squeezed.

"You made it clear that I've become a *distraction*," she reminded him, a hint of bitterness creeping into the words.

"Is that why you're avoiding me? Because I didn't make a more romantic gesture?" His hands were on her before he'd thought through the wisdom of touching her again.

Spinning her away from the fabric display, he turned her to face him, his palms settling into the indent of her waist. Hidden from view, he wrestled with the urge to feel more of her, to mold her to him and put an end to the damnable simmering distraction.

If she'd been anyone else, the next move would have already been made. But this was Addy.

"No. Thinking about romance will not help get us through the next few weeks," she told him evenly. "I'm not one of your girlfriends with a legal agreement you can keep renegotiating, okay? You laid out the terms when you put me on the spot with this engagement. I'm not sure why you think you can keep rewriting those terms to give you more *benefits*."

The bitterness in her voice had vanished. Taking its place was a trace of hurt.

An emotional one-two punch that he'd never intended.

His hands tightened on her waist. His throat dried up.

"You're right." Closing his eyes, he dragged in a deep breath and only succeeded in inhaling a hint of night-blooming roses. "I haven't thought about how this is affecting you. That day you told me you were quitting, I was completely focused on making sure that didn't happen. I came up with the only short-term solution I could."

Dempsey became aware of the sound of a woman's high heels clicking on the concrete floor behind him. She was heading their way.

"Ms. Thibodeaux, do you have any questions—" A tall blonde woman in a dark suit rounded the corner and came into view. "Oh. Hello there." She blushed at the sight of them together, making Dempsey realize how close he'd gotten to Adelaide during this discussion.

How much closer he still wanted to be.

"I put the last sample back," Adelaide told her, edging around Dempsey and straightening. "I'll give you a call once I have a better idea of what I might need."

The woman was already backing away. "Of course! No problem. And congratulations on your engagement."

As soon as the sales clerk disappeared from view, Adelaide swung around to face him.

"So now that you've acknowledged this engagement was a mistake, are you ready to call it off and maybe life can go back to normal?" Her hazel eyes seemed greener in this light. Or maybe it was the combination of anger and challenge firing through them.

"Not until I have a better short-term solution." He understood they needed to have this discussion since this attraction was proving far too distracting at a time when he needed absolute focus. "But you can help me brainstorm alternatives. Over dinner."

Two hours later, Adelaide sat cross-legged on a wooden Adirondack chair behind Dempsey's house overlooking Lake Pontchartrain. A blaze burned in the round fire pit in front of them as they finished a meal of Cajun specialties obtained by Evan from a local restaurant. Adelaide hadn't wanted to risk a public outing, unwilling to smile and lie politely about her engagement to Dempsey when the man was hell-bent on taking their relationship into intimate terrain.

And that's a problem...why? some snide voice in her head kept asking.

Sure, she wanted him. Desperately. But since a corner of her heart had always belonged to him, she feared this new development could have devastating consequences when the time came to return to their regular lives. And the time would come. She'd witnessed Dempsey's parting gifts to his exes enough times to know that relationships came with an expiration date for him. Still, she simmered with thwarted desire. While she finished her meal, she tormented herself with fantasies about touching him. Agreeing to his offer of sensual benefits. Bringing this heat to the boiling point. Even now she wanted to cross over to his chair and take a seat on his lap just to see what would happen.

From her vantage point, his thighs appeared plenty strong enough to bear her weight. Those workouts of his seemed to keep him in optimal shape.

Was she really ready for him to relegate her to friendship for life when she had this opportunity of living with him for the next few weeks? When he'd admitted he couldn't stop thinking about her? She'd nearly melted in her shoes when he'd confessed it at the fabric warehouse.

"Remember when you stole a crawfish for me and I was too afraid to eat it?" she asked, deliberately putting off the more serious conversation he'd promised over dinner.

She wasn't ready to help him brainstorm solutions to their dilemma. And right now she wanted a happy memory to remind her why she put up with him and all that driven, relentless ambition, which kept him from getting too close to anyone. She blamed that and his need to prove himself to his family for his unwillingness to take a risk with the relationship.

Although maybe she just needed to tell herself that to

protect her heart from the more obvious explanation—
that he saw any attraction as a fleeting response doomed
not to last.

"I didn't steal it." He sounded as incensed about it
now as he'd been when he was twelve years old. "If a
crawfish happened to walk over to me, it was exercis-
ing its free will."

Laughing, she set aside the jambalaya that had made
her think of that day. They'd walked to a nearby crawfish festival. When one of the restaurants selling food
at the event refilled its tank of crawfish, a few escap-
ees had headed toward Dempsey and Adelaide, who'd
been drooling over the food from a spot on the pave-
ment nearby.

"I don't know what made you think I would eat a
raw mudbug." She shivered. "Sometimes I still can't
believe I eat them when they're cooked."

"A hungry kid doesn't turn his nose up at much,"
he observed. "And I figured it was only polite to offer
them to you before I helped myself."

Adelaide had never gone hungry the way Dempsey
sometimes had. His mother could be kind when she
was drug-free, but even then the woman had never had
any extra money thanks to her habit. When she'd been
using more, she'd even forgotten about Dempsey for
days on end.

"You were very good to me." When Adelaide looked
back on those days, she could almost forget about how
much he'd shut her out of his personal life since then.

He stared into the flames dancing in the fire pit.

"I still try to be good to you, Addy."

She bit back the sharp retort that came to mind, pur-
posely focusing on the friendship they used to have so

as not to bad-mouth the turn things had taken over the past five years.

"I take it you don't agree?" he asked.

"We've had a strict work-only relationship for years." She traced patterns in the condensation on her iced tea glass. "You convinced me to take this job that furthered your career while delaying mine. You've ignored our friendship for years at a time, going so far as referring to me as a 'tool for greater productivity.'" She wanted to stop there. But now that the brakes were off, she found it difficult to put them back on. "Or maybe you think it's *kind* of you to toy with the chemistry between us, pretending to feel the same heat that I do and using it to your own ends to convince me to stay?"

She knew she'd admitted too much, but sitting in the dark under the bayou stars seemed to coax the truth from her. Besides, if she didn't put herself on the line with him now when he'd admitted to being "distracted" by her, she might never have another chance to find out where all that simmering attraction could lead.

"Damn, Addy." He whistled low and sat up straighter in his chair, his elbows on his knees. Firelight cast stark shadows on his face. "You must think I'm some kind of arrogant, selfish ass. Do you really think that's how I perceive things? That I created a position for you just to benefit me?"

"You're putting words in my mouth."

"Nothing you didn't imply." He rose to his feet, his agitation apparent as he paced a circle around his vacated chair. "And I can assure you that you were not the most obvious choice to work with me in this capacity. There aren't many assistant coaches who bring an administrative aide with them when they take a new job, but I did it just the same because you needed a job at the time. And I'm the only coach in the league with a female personal assistant, so I'm breaking all kinds of ground there."

"You can't honestly suggest that you created the job for me to further my career. I wanted to be an artist."

"Yes. An artist. And your work led you to a studio in an even worse part of town than where we grew up. A place I warned you not to take. I offered to rent another space for you. But then—"

"The break-in." She didn't want to think about that night when gang members, high on heaven knew what, had broken into the studio and threatened her.

They'd destroyed her paintings when they'd realized there was nothing of value in the place to steal. Then they'd casually discussed the merits of physically assaulting her before one of them got a text that they needed to be elsewhere. The three of them had disappeared into the night while she'd remained paralyzed with fear long afterward.

"Those bastards threatened you. And I suggested every plan under the sun to help you, Addy, but you were too stubborn and proud to let me do anything."

Crickets chirped in the silence that followed. A log shifted in the fire pit, sending sparks flying.

"You wanted to build me a studio in the country." She recalled a fax from an architect with the plans for such a building, including a state-of-the-art security system. "How on earth could I have ever repaid you for such a thing? I was barely out of college."

"Like I said. Too stubborn." He spread his hands wide. "I was just a few years out of college myself and I was dealing with a lot of family expectations. The studio would have been easy for me to give you and I was happy to do it, but you wouldn't hear of it."

"I'd never take something for nothing. And don't you blame me for that, because you wouldn't either if our positions were reversed." Maybe she hadn't let herself remember that time in detail because it had taken a long time to recover from the emotional trauma of that night.

Seeing her canvases hacked to bits had been different than having her computer stolen or her phone smashed. Her art was an extension of her, a place where she poured her heart.

"So I gave you a job. That, you would accept."

"And now, years after the fact, I'm still supposed to kiss your feet for the opportunity?" She shot out of her chair, a restless energy taking hold as she closed the distance between them.

"Absolutely not."

His quick agreement didn't come close to satisfying her.

"I worked hard in an industry I knew nothing about," she pressed. "I left my home and everything I knew to go to Atlanta with you." Her first task had been finding housing for them.

Relocating to a new city had been so simple with Dempsey's seemingly limitless resources and connections.

Unlike starting over in New Orleans, which had seemed impossible after her sense of safety had been shredded and her body of work reduced to scraps.

"Yes. And you proved yourself invaluable almost right away. My work was easier with your help. You never needed direction and understood me even on days

I was so terse and exhausted I could only snap out a few words of instructions for you."

"I had a long history of interpreting you." A wry grin tugged at her lips, but she wasn't going to let nostalgia cloud her vision of him. Of them.

"But we'd scarcely seen each other for a decade." He reached toward her, as if to stroke her cheek, but he must have thought better of it when his hand fell to his side. "I was surprised how well we got back into sync."

"You might be more surprised to know how much more in sync we could be." The words leaped from her mouth.

One moment they were in her head. The next they were in the air, with no way to recapture them.

She saw the instant that full understanding hit him. The instant he heard the proposition underlying those words. His gaze shifted to her mouth, the heat in his eyes like a laser in its intensity.

"Of course it would *not* surprise me. That's exactly what I've been trying to tell you." He focused all his attention on her. "You've occupied every second of my thoughts today. You've got me so damn distracted, I can hardly think about football."

Still he didn't move toward her. Didn't give in to the current that leaped back and forth between them. Her cells practically strained toward the sound of his voice.

"Then, maybe you ought to call off this engagement charade before you tank a season that means everything to you." She wouldn't make the first move again. Being impulsive with him the night before had only complicated things between them.

"I don't think so." He reached behind her and tugged a pin from the knot at the back of her head. Then, sifting through the half-fallen mass, he found two more and pulled them free.

Her hair tumbled to her bare shoulders and covered her arms. She shivered despite the warmth of the night, awareness flooding through her like high tide.

"Why not?" Her voice rasped low from the effort of not stepping closer. She wanted him to touch her the way he had the night before. Craved the feel of his body against hers.

"Because I have a better solution for all this distraction you're causing." He combed his fingers through the ends of her hair, smoothing it along her back.

Sensation shimmered over her skin, nerve endings dancing to life. Desire pooled in her belly as her gaze roamed over his powerful arms and shoulders, the solid wall of his chest that would be warm to her touch.

"A way to stop all this distraction?" She needed to know what he was thinking before her thoughts smoldered away in the blaze erupting between them.

"I'm beginning to think that's a lost cause after last night." His hands moved to her hips as he stepped into her space, crowding her in the most delicious possible way. "That dress you wore last night flipped some kind of switch in my head and I can't stop thinking about this spot." He palmed the front of her thigh. "Right here."

Her breath caught on a hard gasp. Pleasure spiked. Her breasts beaded under the bodice of her dress.

"Do you remember where I mean?" His eyes were dark and lit by firelight, reflecting the bright orange flames beside them. He traced a pattern on the front of her leg, fingering gently. "There was a sheer place in the lace. Here."

He increased the pressure of his touch and she

couldn't swallow a strangled sound in the back of her throat. He hadn't even kissed her yet and she was utterly mesmerized.

"I remember." Her words were a breathless whisper as she steadied herself against his shoulders, anchoring her quivering body with his strength.

"If I'm a bad friend to you, Addy, you only have that dress to blame." He shifted his hold on her to align their hips, allowing her to feel how much he wanted her. "But I damn well can't resist any longer."

Seven

Dempsey's control had snapped the second she'd suggested they could be even more in sync. He'd been hanging on by a thread before that moment, willing himself not to think about the tender brush of her lips on his the night before. Not to think about that damn siren's dress she'd worn or the way she'd melted in his arms.

So by the time she'd made that one coy, flirtatious taunt, his restraint had simply incinerated.

From that moment on, he'd been plagued with sweaty visions of them moving together in perfect sensual accord. Now that he had his hands on her, molding her sweet, curvy body to his, he didn't have a prayer of putting a lid back on this combustible attraction.

He kissed her. Hard. With deliberate purpose. Need. Seeking entrance, he explored every nuance of her mouth, claiming it with a hunger and thoroughness he couldn't hold back. The way she opened for him, swayed into him, encouraged him all the more.

Unleashed, his emotions fired through the kiss until he all but devoured her. She clutched his shoulders, her nails biting ever so slightly into his skin through his shirt. He wished he could torch their clothes so he could feel the sting of that touch without barrier.

He bent to nuzzle her neck, tasting the skin all along her throat and under her ear until he found the source of her fragrance. The scent of roses made him throb with teeth-jarring need. He nipped and licked his way down her collarbone along the strap of her dress and peeled the fabric free. He had to feel more of her.

But right before he helped himself to one of her breasts, he remembered they were still outdoors. And even though it was nighttime, the fire might make them visible to one of the houses dotting the lake if someone was so inclined to spy. The porches of plenty of coastal homes were furnished with telescopes.

"I want to take you inside." He nudged the strap of her dress back up her shoulder, his hand unsteady and his breath uneven. The ache from wanting her still heated his veins.

"I want to take you anywhere I can have you." She loosened her hold on him as she edged back a step. "So that's definitely fine with me."

Her words fanned the flames hotter inside him. Aching to have her, he swept her up in his arms and charged over the lawn toward the house.

"Your room is closer." He said it to himself as much as her, directing his steps toward the downstairs bedroom. "But the condoms are all upstairs." He changed direction, cursing himself for the mansion's extravagant square footage when it delayed having Adelaide.

She nipped at his neck while he covered the distance, those delectable breasts of hers pressed tight to his chest as she clutched him. She made a luscious armful, her thighs draped over one arm while her hip grazed the erection that had hounded him the better part of the day.

"I can't wait to feel you without the barrier of clothes," she murmured against his ear, her breath puffing a silken caress along his skin.

"That's good." He ground the words out between clenched teeth as he finally reached the door to his suite. "Because I don't think we're going to leave this room until the game on Sunday."

He needed to wear himself out with her. To excise this hunger spilling over into every aspect of his life until all he could think about was Adelaide.

Setting her on her feet, he backed her into the nearest wall, yearning to feel more of her. Light spilled into the room from low-wattage sconces on either side of the bed that came on automatically at sunset. He toed the door shut behind them and took another valuable second to flip the lock into place. Then all of his focus returned to Adelaide.

Immersing his hands in all that long, caramel-colored hair of hers, he shifted the length of it over one shoulder in a silky veil. His body pinned hers in place, hips sinking into hers where they fit best.

He was dying to have her. It was as if he'd been holding back for years instead of days, and maybe subconsciously he had been. That friendship wall could be a strong one. Mistresses were plentiful. Friends, true friends, were few. But the time for restraint was long gone as he tugged the straps of her thin sundress down and exposed a pretty turquoise-colored bra that wouldn't be nearly as enticing as what was underneath. Applying his hands to the hooks, he swept that aside, too, so he could get his mouth around the tight buds of dark pink nipples he'd felt right through her clothes.

Her back arched to give him better access, her body straining toward his while he laved and licked at one and then the other. She made soft sexy sounds that told him how much she liked what he was doing, and her hands worked the buttons on his shirt until she was touching bare skin. He hauled the shirt off his shoulders and let it slide to the floor, his eyes never leaving her. With her dress tugged down and all that goddess hair draped over her shoulders, she made one hell of a vision.

Lifting her against him, he slid a hand up her skirt to wrap her leg around his waist. Positioned that way, the vulnerable, hot core of her came up against his rock-hard erection. She shuddered against him, a subtle vibration he felt right there, a sensation so damn good he cupped her hips and moved her against him again and again. A sensual ride he wanted to give her for real.

"That feels…" Her words broke on a small cry of pleasure as she braced herself on his shoulders.

"Tell me." He wanted to know everything she liked. Exactly how she liked it.

While he'd always striven to pleasure the women in his bed, this was different. He needed this night to be perfect because this was Adelaide and *she* was different. So much more important to him.

And he wasn't ready to think about what that meant or all the ways that was going to complicate things for them.

"It feels so good." Her eyes flipped open long enough

for him to see the haze of desire there, her gaze unfocused. "I'm so close. Already."

Knowing that only cranked him higher. He kept up the friction beginning to torment him and fastened his lips back on one breast. He drew on it. Hard. Then, finding the edge of her panties with one hand, he slid beneath the satin to stroke the drenched feminine folds. Once. Twice.

She came apart with a high cry she muffled against his shoulder. The force of it, combined with the way she went boneless in his arms, made him sway back on his feet a little.

Damn. He used that moment to watch her, to soak up the vision she made with her cheeks suffused with color and her chest heaving with all that sensation.

Giving her a moment—giving himself one, too—he tried to catch his breath before he carried her over to the bed and deposited her there. His own release was close and he hadn't even taken off his pants. Leaving her just long enough to retrieve a box of condoms from the bathroom cabinet, he dropped it on the nightstand.

Then he went to work on his belt while he watched her slide off her heels. He dropped his pants while she wriggled out of her dress. He was left wearing only his boxers at the same time she wore nothing but turquoise-colored satin panties.

"I'll show you mine if you show me yours," she dared him, hooking a finger in the lace waistband about as substantial as a shoelace.

He slid off the boxers.

"I'm going to see yours, all right," he warned her, edging a knee onto the bed and stretching out over her. "Up close and personal."

She let go of the panties, her hand moving to his chest as he shifted closer.

"Oh?" Her breathless question told him exactly how much she liked that idea. "Well, I'm going to revisit on you all the same pleasure that you give me." She arched an eyebrow at the sensual promise.

Laying a hand on her hip, he slipped the satin down her thighs and off.

"Not a chance. This isn't like a favor where you can keep an accounting. In this bed, I get to give and give and give all that I want." He stroked the soft curls just above her sex, sliding touches lower and lower while she drew in a breath between her teeth.

"Dempsey." She arched her hips toward him, a silent plea.

One he was powerless to resist.

Parting her thighs, he made room for himself there. She watched him with wide eyes, biting the soft fullness of her lower lip while he found a condom and opened the packet. She stole it away from him, rolling it into place herself and positioning him where she wanted.

Where they both wanted.

When he entered her, she tightened her grip on him. Her arms wrapped around his shoulders. Legs tightened around his waist. And her inner muscles squeezed him with sensual pulls that had him gritting his teeth against the sweetly erotic feel of one hundred percent Adelaide.

For a long moment, he held himself still, breathing in the scent of her hair and giving her time to adjust to him. When he thought he could move again without unmanning himself, he levered up on his arms and began a slow, steady rhythm. Addy held herself still for a moment, and then, as if she'd just been waiting for the right time to join him, she swiveled her hips in a way that rocked him.

Heat blazed up his spine as she undulated beneath him, meeting his thrusts and making him see stars. She locked her ankles behind him, her heat, her softness and her scent surrounding him. He wanted to draw this out, to make the pleasure go on and on, to explore every facet of what she liked. But not this time. Not now when just being inside her was enough to send him hurtling over the edge.

Next time, he'd find some self-control. Some way to make the pleasure last. Right now the need to come inside her was the most primal urge he'd ever felt. He closed his eyes, cued in on her breathing and synced his movements, causing her to gasp and arch. He moved faster, needing to focus solely on her. On pleasuring her.

He wouldn't let himself go until then.

She called his name with a hoarse cry as her whole body went taut. Her release pulsated through her and freed his. He kissed her to silence, the shout poised in his throat as wave after wave of pleasure pounded through him. The moment went on and on until they were both spent and lying side by side, their breathing erratic and heartbeats pounding crazy rhythms. He knew because one of his hands rested on her throat, where he could feel her pulse hammer.

She must know, too, because her hand lay on his chest, where his heart thrummed so hard it felt as though it wanted out.

Long minutes passed before their skin began to cool and Dempsey thought he could move again. He drew her into his arms and stroked her hair, smoothing tangles and skimming it to one side of her beautiful body.

"I'm speechless," she murmured, her breath a soft huff on his chest.

"We could make talking optional for the next few hours," he suggested, already wanting her again.

She peered up at him through long lashes. "Save all our energy for the important things?"

"Exactly." He cupped her cheek and tilted her face to kiss her. "You can practically read my mind anyhow. You can probably guess what I'd like to do next."

She sidled closer, her hips stirring him to life with a speed he hadn't experienced since his teens.

"I have an excellent idea. But I stopped being your dutiful assistant when you gave me the day off. So I won't be fulfilling your every need tonight." She ran a lazy hand up his biceps and onto his chest. Then trailed her nails lightly down the center of his sternum.

"No?" His voice rasped on a dry note.

"I might give a few orders of my own," she teased.

"Is that what I do? Order you around?" He found a ticklish spot on her side and made her laugh.

"Definitely." She gripped his wrists and pinned them to the bed. Climbing on top of him, she let all that glorious hair fall around him. "Now it's my turn."

Adelaide couldn't resist teasing him. She stared down into Dempsey's impossibly handsome face and wondered how long he would let her play this game.

Judging from the impressive erection resting on his abs, he was liking it well enough so far.

"I can't imagine what you'd ask me to do when I've already put so much thought into pleasing you, Ms. Thibodeaux." His dark eyes wandered over her in the most flattering way.

"I already like your deferential tone." She kissed his cheek and brushed her breasts against it. "Why don't you tell me about this effort you say you've put into pleasing me? I'd love to hear all about that."

Kissing her way down his chest, she paused now and again to look up at him. Make sure he was still watching. Still liking what she was doing. Because honestly, she had little enough experience with men, and none with a man like Dempsey. She could only trust her instincts to guide her and have fun with him in this rare moment to play and tease.

And enjoy his sinfully delicious body.

"I've taken all my cues from you tonight," he informed her, his muscles flexing under her as she slid down him to kiss his abs.

"How do you mean?" She peered up to find him shoving a pillow under his head.

Making himself comfortable? Or getting ready to watch the show? Nerves danced along her skin, mingling with anticipation. When he put his hands behind his head, it was a devastating look for a man with his build, emphasizing the way his upper body tapered to narrow hips.

"You get a sexy look in your eyes when you're thinking wicked thoughts, Addy. I know that's when to make my move."

"A sexy look?" She stroked a light touch up the hard length of him.

He hissed a breath between his teeth. "Definitely." He shifted under her, his whole body tensing.

She climbed back up him to whisper in his ear, "I've never done this before. Feel free to offer instruction." She paused to kiss his lips and wander her way down his body again, taking his incoherent groan as a good sign that he was on board with her plan.

She listened to every intake of his breath, repeating the things he liked best. When she traced the indents between his abs with her tongue, he almost came off the bed.

That was when she experimented with how she touched him, discovering it was easy to know what he liked. Tasting him received wholehearted approval. In fact, the more of him that she took into her mouth, the more encouraging his reaction.

"Addy." His tone warned her more than his words. And he would have hauled her up to kiss him if she hadn't paused to remind him who was in charge.

"Let go," she commanded, meeting his gaze one last time before she returned to the kisses he liked so well.

When his release came, she savored it, loving that rare moment of seeing him lose control. Of knowing she'd given him that pleasure.

But when the hot pulses halted and a final groan ripped from his throat, Dempsey reached for her and dragged her back up his body. His golden-brown gaze seared her. As if he'd taken her game as a personal challenge, he settled between her thighs and kissed her.

The sharp jolt of sensual pleasure was like an electric shock, rippling through every part of her. He dipped one shoulder beneath her thigh and then the other, finding just the right angle to slowly drive her to the edge of madness. Each stroke of his tongue sent quivery ribbons of pleasure to her belly. Fingers twisting in the sheets, she held on as he nipped and licked, making her fly apart in hard spasms that went on and on.

She wanted to say something about that, the intensity of the orgasm unlike anything she'd ever felt. But the hungry look still lurked in his eyes as he stretched out over her, kissing her mouth while he found another condom and seated himself deep inside her.

Any words she'd been about to speak dried up in her throat. All she could do was hold on and trust him to take care of her body, which was in the grip of a hunger that seemed bigger than both of them. Tucking her cheek against his chest, she closed her eyes and got lost in the feel of him inside her.

Dempsey. Reynaud.

She felt as if all her life had led to this moment. This joining. This wild heat that shook her to her core. And when at last he found his release, taking her with him yet again, Adelaide kissed him hard in a tangle of tongues and pleasure.

Afterward, she could barely move, but she didn't need to. Every part of her felt sated. Happy. And— at least in the physical sense—well loved. She knew they'd taken an irreparable step away from friendship toward something potentially more dangerous. But with the heavy feeling in her limbs and Dempsey's naked body wrapped around hers, she refused to have any regrets tonight. They would come, she guessed, as sure as the sunrise.

For now, however, she was going to squeeze every moment of pleasure she could out of this fake engagement and their time together. There was always a chance Dempsey could learn to care about her as more than a friend before their four weeks were up.

If sex was a way to make that happen, she would just have to sacrifice her body for the greater good.

And if her gamble didn't pay off? Adelaide would

have some incredible memories to keep her warm at night. She told herself it was a good plan. The only plan she had. But a little voice in her head kept reminding her that Dempsey didn't have affairs without an expiration date. How many times had Adelaide shipped off one of those extravagant tennis bracelets to a former lover?

She ought to know better than anyone. The only reason Dempsey had initiated this unwise relationship was because she was quitting soon. Yet knowing how their affair would end before it happened wasn't going to make it any easier when Dempsey walked away.

Eight

When Dempsey's alarm chimed before dawn, he slammed the off button and hoped it hadn't woken Adelaide. They hadn't slept much with the fever for each other burning in their blood. He didn't want to wear her out, but the last time they'd been together had been her idea after they'd headed into the kitchen to refuel after midnight. She'd made crepes from scratch and they'd been amazing. Including the part when she'd taunted him to find the hint of raspberry sauce she'd dabbed on her bare skin while he wasn't looking.

That game had ended deliciously, but it had required a shower, where he'd gotten to wash her long hair himself. He'd wanted her then, too, when he'd carried her damp, freshly washed body back to his bed. But he hadn't wanted to exhaust her.

Studying her face in the shadows cast from the

bathroom light—they'd fallen asleep without shutting it off—Dempsey wondered what it would be like to work side by side now that they'd shared this incredible night. He'd never touched a woman he did business with. It was a rule he'd kept all through the years as he'd learned about the Reynauds' shipping empire from his grandfather, unwilling to have anyone draw a comparison between Dempsey's personal ethics and his parents.

"I can hear you thinking," Adelaide whispered, her eyes still closed.

"Maybe I'm thinking about how good you taste." He stroked her hair, still damp in places from their late-night shower. In other spots, strands had turned kinky, a phenomenon he remembered from when they were kids and she'd let it run wild.

He kissed her bare shoulder, breathing in the scent of roses that lingered even now that it mixed with his soap.

"My female intuition suggests there's more going on in your brain than that." She captured his hand where he touched her and threaded her fingers between his. "Do you really need to go to work already?"

"No. But I received a text last night from Evan that one of the players I cut in training camp—Marcus Wheelan—was picked up by the cops for getting into a fight in a local bar. I need to talk to him. See if I can get through to him before he heads down a path that he can't recover from." Dempsey had been saved from choosing that kind of life by a fluke of birth, a lucky chance. But if Theo Reynaud hadn't shown up to pluck Dempsey out of his old life, what were the chances that it would be Dempsey who spent the occasional Friday night in jail?

Or worse.

"Won't that attract the kind of publicity you don't want around the team?" Adelaide shifted, turning to meet his gaze.

"I'll get a lawyer to look at the bail situation and pull Marcus out of there so I can speak to him privately." Dempsey wasn't clear on the charges yet, but hoped they were no more serious than disorderly conduct or resisting arrest—the kinds of things police leveled at drunken, noisy athletes.

But according to Evan, who kept in touch with a lot of the players who'd been invited to training camp, Marcus had been out with a rough group. He'd taken it hard when he hadn't made the Hurricanes' regular-season roster after getting cut by a West Coast team last spring.

"That's good of you." She feathered a light touch along his cheek, her expression troubled. "I hope he listens."

"Me, too." He kissed her forehead and waged an inner battle not to slide his hands beneath the sheets and lose himself in her one more time. "And I hope you can get some more sleep."

She ignored his efforts at restraint, sidling over to him and slipping a slender thigh between his.

"I'll sleep better knowing you left the house happy." Her whispered words were like a drug, finding their way into his bloodstream and sending a fresh wave of heat through him.

"I could get used to this in a hurry." He gripped her hips and molded her curves to his, her breasts flattening against his chest.

He needed to be inside her, exploring her heat and hearing her soft moans in his ear. He'd never felt this way about a woman before, when every time with her made him want her even more. Again and again. He'd barely be able to walk by tomorrow at this rate.

But he didn't even care.

She pressed kisses along his shoulder and skimmed a hand down his chest. Lower.

"Good. Because I want you thinking about me at work today. And I want you to rush home early because you need to be with me all over again."

They both knew that was exactly what would happen, too. Already he couldn't imagine spending hours away from her. For a moment, he felt a pang of conscience that he was allowing this kind of relationship to grow unchecked, the kind where they could lose themselves in each other completely. He wondered how he would handle it once that heat finally burned itself out, but far more important, he should be thinking about Adelaide.

What would it do to her?

Not ready to consider that right now when they were only just beginning to discover all the ways they could drive one another to new heights of pleasure, Dempsey shut down his thoughts. He let the magic of Adelaide's touch carry him into a sensual world that was all their own.

Afterward, Adelaide walked along the lakeshore at sunrise as Dempsey showered and prepared to drive into the training facility. The grounds all around the Reynaud homes were breathtaking, the landscaping exotic and a little wild. She'd never gardened much herself, but she knew well how fast things grew in this kind of weather, and that it would take a whole fleet of full-time gardeners to meticulously maintain all of the dense plantings around the low-rock retaining walls and fountains, or the vines crawling up some of the outbuildings.

And, to her way of thinking, the rich greenery and abundance of flowers looked more natural than precisely trimmed boxwoods or well-spaced English gardens. Turning her attention back to her path along the lake, she spied a feminine figure walking toward her.

Princess Erika Mitras was engaged to Dempsey's older brother, Gervais, and she'd recently moved into his home near Dempsey's place. Adelaide had met her a few weeks ago when she'd first arrived and been thoroughly dazzled. Refined, royal and incredibly lovely, Erika was the kind of woman who would always draw stares, but there was much more to her than that. She'd served in her country's military, defying her parents' wishes to fulfill a call to civic duty.

Smiling, the princess navigated the walking path in glittery gold sandals and a gauzy white sundress. Her cool Nordic looks and platinum blond hair were shielded by a wide-brimmed hat.

"Good morning," Adelaide greeted her. "Did you happen to see the sunrise?"

Even now, the sky streaked with bright pink light.

"I was awake and waiting for it." She covered a yawn. "It is the curse of pregnancy that I can only sleep when I do not want to."

Adelaide turned to walk in the same direction as the other woman. In the distance, she saw a shirtless Gervais running toward them.

"Well, you look fantastic for someone who didn't sleep well."

"Maybe it is the pregnancy glow," Erika said wryly.

"Or else just plain happiness. I cannot believe how lucky I am to have Gervais in my life. I told him how beignets settle my stomach in the morning, and now he has fresh, warm beignets for me every day."

"How thoughtful. And romantic." Adelaide wondered if Dempsey would do things like that for the mother of his child one day. She paused to pick up a piece of driftwood with an interesting shape, thinking she might find a spot for it in one of the gardens.

"True. Although that is why I have taken to walking in the mornings. I will need the exercise to bear the many, many pounds I plan to gain over the next months."

Adelaide laughed. "You must have so many plans to make to prepare for your baby."

"Babies, actually. Did you not hear that I am having twins?" Erika rested a hand on Adelaide's forearm, a friendly touch that made her realize how few close female friends she had in her life.

Of course, she'd been living and breathing work and football these past four years.

"Oh, Erika." Adelaide's chest ached with a longing for the kind of happiness this woman had found. "How incredible. Congratulations." She hugged her gently. "Please, please let me know if there's anything I can do to help."

"Gervais already treats me as though I am carrying the weight of the world on my shoulders." Her good humor was contagious. "I have to tell him I am a healthy, strong woman. I do not need to put my feet up every moment of the day." She leaned close to lower her voice. "I am telling him that an active sex life will lead to happier babies."

"Well, it must have worked." She pointed to where Gervais had paused to do a cycle of push-ups along the path. "He looks as if he's in training for a marathon."

"As I said, I am a lucky woman." Erika winked and shared her plans for decorating a nursery as they walked.

Adelaide listened attentively, all the while wondering what it would be like to be expecting a first child. She had never stopped to think much about babies, since she had never come close to finding a lasting love relationship and, of course, that needed to happen first.

But all the talk of babies and parenting tugged at her heart. She couldn't help but wonder what would happen if she were to become pregnant. Would Dempsey be excited? More likely he would not be pleased. He'd made it clear their relationship would have boundaries. For years, they had just been friends. Then, she'd been his assistant.

Now she was his lover.

After that? She feared she would be very much alone.

When Dempsey left the house that morning, he spotted Adelaide down by lake, walking with Gervais's future wife. For all that Adelaide had resisted getting close with his family, she looked comfortable enough, pausing in her walk to give the other woman a hug.

The sight did something peculiar to his insides. She was so naturally warmhearted and caring. Of course she would befriend the pregnant foreign princess who must be struggling to adjust to life in New Orleans as she prepared to be a mother.

Dempsey crossed the driveway to reach the detached garage when he caught sight of a familiar figure jogging toward him, his only neighbor right now while Henri spent the season in the Garden District house with his wife.

"Gervais." Dempsey lifted a hand in greeting.

The eldest Reynaud brother, like Dempsey, had walked away from football after college because of injuries. He still ran every day, though, and Dempsey had caught sight of him in the players' gym after-hours some nights, working out to the point of exhaustion. Dempsey had never fully understood his brother's demons, since Gervais had always been the heir to a billion-dollar corporation and he'd been born with the innate business sense to run it well. But then, Gervais had always been the most coolly controlled one of them.

"Congratulations on your engagement." Sweating and shirtless, he slowed his pace to run in place. "Sorry I haven't been by to welcome Adelaide to the family. It's been a busy week in the front office while we prepare for the regular season to start."

"I wouldn't have chosen the week of our home opener for the engagement announcement if it hadn't been necessary." If Addy hadn't decided to quit on him, that is. Although it was tough to regret her decision now, knowing it had led to the most incredible night of his life.

Gervais raised a brow. "Necessary? As in, I won't be the only one trying to navigate the challenges of fatherhood next spring?"

"No." Dempsey hit the remote to raise the door to the farthest right bay in the garage. "You're on your own with that—double dose. Adelaide and I got engaged for different reasons, but the timing was unavoidable."

"Spoken like the romantic soul you've always been," Gervais said drily, clapping him on the shoulder. "But at least Adelaide understands you well. You two want to come up to the house for dinner tonight? Erika is used to having her sisters around. I know she would be glad to get to know her future sister-in-law."

"I'll check with Adelaide, but given how they seem to be enjoying their conversation on the beach now, I think that'll be a good plan." Surprised at the invitation— they'd never extended such invites to one another as bachelors—Dempsey wondered for a split second how family dynamics would change with women around. But then, that wasn't really a concern for now, since Adelaide wouldn't be under his roof for long. He would return to his usual role as the Reynaud black sheep then.

"Good. We can sneak away to watch some game film after dessert." Gervais started jogging again, backward. "You can let me in on the highlights of Sunday's game plan."

"Of course." So it would be a working dinner. Still, he appreciated the offer. "I'll text you once I speak to Adelaide."

Since the four Reynaud brothers had gone off to college, they hadn't spent much time together outside of family gatherings that their grandfather insisted on. Even now, Leon was the most likely to bring them together. Dempsey hated to think that their grandfather's decline in health would be the next thing to put Gervais, Dempsey, Henri and Jean-Pierre in the same room together.

Maybe tonight would be a step toward having a stronger relationship with Gervais—they had a working partnership to protect in the Hurricanes if nothing else. The only drawback would be that Dempsey would have to share Adelaide for a few hours, and with their time together limited, he didn't like the idea of giving up any of it.

They'd been together intimately for less than twenty-four hours and already Adelaide had gotten under his skin deeper than any other woman he'd ever known.

"I love your earrings." Erika lifted a hand toward Adelaide's ear as they sat outside by the pool behind Gervais's breathtaking home that evening. "May I?"

They were sipping virgin margaritas under a pergola heavy with bright pink bougainvillea. Adelaide had mixed feelings about the evening, since getting closer to Dempsey's family would only make their breakup more difficult when it happened. But visiting with Gervais's fiancée this morning and this evening had been surprisingly fun. There was nothing pretentious about this Vikingesque princess who, apparently, was one of five daughters in a family of deposed royalty from a tiny kingdom near Norway.

Their casual outdoor dinner had made Adelaide all the more committed to building a business and a life for herself outside the male-dominated world of football. She craved more girl time.

"Of course." She scooted closer on the massive side-by-side lounger they shared, since Erika had wanted to put her feet up and insisted Adelaide should, too. "These are a sample from an accessory collection I hope to design for female sports fans."

"Sports fans?" Erika frowned, a pout that didn't come close to diminishing her stunning good looks. "They do not look like sports paraphernalia."

Close up, Adelaide marveled at the other woman's skin tone. But then, maybe living so far north the sun couldn't wreak the same kind of havoc. She'd rather take the freckles, she decided, than live for months in the cold.

"That's because they are intended to offset other team-oriented clothes. Most women don't want to dress in head-to-toe gear like a player. So I have some pieces that are very focused on team logos, and some accessories that pick up the colors or motifs in a more subtle way so that fans can be coordinated without being cartoonish."

"So when I buy Henri's jersey to wear—just to tease Gervais, of course—" she gave Adelaide a conspiratorial grin as she released the jewelry "—I can wear gorgeous black-and-gold earrings with it."

"Exactly." Sipping her icy-cold cocktail that made good use of fresh oranges and limes, Adelaide winked at her new friend. "And how can your future husband argue when the jersey has the Reynaud name on it?"

"There is a bit of competition among them. Have you noticed this?"

Adelaide nearly choked on her drink after the unexpected laugh. "I've noticed. You'd be surprised to know it was even worse when they were teenagers."

"Tell me." Erika peered over her shoulder where the brothers had sat a few minutes before. "It is safe. They are watching their games on television."

"When I first met Dempsey's brothers, I was thirteen." It was a year after he'd been living with the Reynauds and she'd been so excited that he'd invited her to his fourteenth birthday party. The day had been a disaster for many reasons, mostly because she'd realized that her friend had become someone else since leaving

St. Roch Avenue. "And they knew I was Dempsey's friend, so they decided to vie for my attention."

"Because when you have a sibling, you enjoy irritating them. Trust me, I understand that part a little too well."

As an only child, Adelaide hadn't. She wished she'd understood because she'd handled the attention all wrong.

"One of them decided they should have a race to see who was fastest. On that particular day, fastest was synonymous with best."

"I would bet Gervais won because he was eldest." Erika sipped her drink, adjusting her blue-and-white sundress around her legs as she shifted to her side.

"Well, he would have, except Dempsey tripped him." She'd been so disappointed he'd cheated that she'd failed to see the significance of him needing to win for her. At least, that was what she'd decided it meant later.

"Of course he did. You were *his* friend." She stirred the ice in her glass with the red straw and waved over a maid who had emerged from the house to pick up the dishes from their dessert. "May we have some waters?" she asked the server, passing off her glass. "And the men are in Gervais's study. I believe he keeps brandy in there, but will you see if they need anything?"

The woman nodded before disappearing into the house.

"I didn't really understand how competitive they were at the time. I just thought it meant Dempsey had turned into a bully and I spent the party being kind to Gervais."

Erika laughed. "So he won after all." Her blue eyes sparkled. "What a clever clan we are marrying into,

Adelaide." She reached to squeeze her hand. "I'm so glad I will have a new sister here."

Adelaide swallowed, her throat and eyes suddenly burning. Tricking nice people did not sit well with her. She blinked fast.

"I've never had a sister." She cleared her throat, grateful for the maid's return so she could accept a fresh glass of sparkling water with lime. "Let's not be competitive, though," she added.

"Deal." Erika clinked her water glass with Adelaide's. "Now, will you order me some of your earrings? And whatever else I need to be a stylish sports fan?"

"Of course." Flattered, Adelaide wondered if she would still want the items once her engagement was broken. "Thank you."

"But I'll need some things in blue and white, too, in addition to the Hurricanes gear."

"Blue and white?" Puzzled, she turned to see Gervais and Dempsey headed down the steps from an outdoor deck on an upper story.

"Some days I'll have to root for Jean-Pierre's team, of course. He *is* family." She pantomimed zipping her lips and throwing away the key.

The princess was a firecracker in couture clothes. It made Adelaide happy for Gervais, who seemed as if he could use more fun in his life. But as they said their good-nights and walked back across the landscaped properties separating their homes, she couldn't help a hollow feeling in her chest.

"Thank you for spending time with my family." Dempsey slid an arm around her waist as they passed a line of Italian cypress trees and rounded a courtyard with a fountain at the center.

"You don't have to thank me. I had fun." She held her hand out as they neared the fountain so she could feel a hint of the cool spray drifting on the breeze.

"Did you?" He halted their steps on the gray cobblestones and tipped her chin up. "You look troubled."

She took comfort in his concern. "Erika was so kind to me. It feels wrong to deceive them about us." She searched his expression for clues to what he was thinking.

"An unfortunate necessity," he admitted, his handsome face revealing nothing while his hands smoothed down her back in a reassuring rub. "What do you think of Erika?"

"I like her. She's witty and sharp. I think she will liven up Gervais's world, and I bet she'll be a fabulous mother."

"That's good. He deserves to be happy." Palming the small of her back, he turned her toward his house again.

"Why? What do *you* think of her?" She knew Dempsey well enough to understand when he wasn't saying everything on his mind.

"I didn't get to speak with her one-on-one the way you did, but I trust your judgment. I researched her when Gervais announced the engagement, and her family—for all that she's royalty—has come close to bankruptcy in the past. So I wondered—"

"That's a horrible thought." Defensiveness surged at the insult to their lovely hostess. "And incredibly cynical."

"My grandfather taught us to be wary of fortune hunters from an early age." He kept to the cobblestone path until they reached his driveway. "Said he worked too hard building the company to have it torn apart by that kind of infighting."

"So is it safe to assume your brothers and grandfather are all reviewing my financial information this week?" She didn't like the idea of being held up to scrutiny for a fake engagement. She quickened her step as they neared the front door. "Because if a foreign princess rouses suspicion of gold digging, I can only imagine what the Reynauds think of a struggling artist from your old neighborhood."

"No one questions our relationship when we've been friends for more than half my lifetime." He circled around so he could hold the door open for her. "Every single member of my family knows you're important to me."

Some of the frustration eased out of her at the reassurance. She was important to him. But would she remain that way once she was no longer his fiancée?

A ball of panic bounced through her at the thought, but now they were inside and Dempsey's golden-brown eyes were already alight with desire as he stared down at her in the foyer.

"All through dinner, I was thinking about the moment when that door would close behind us." He crossed the polished Italian marble floor to eliminate the distance between them. "You know what else I was thinking about?"

"No." Her heartbeat did a crazy dance, and she was all too willing to let go of her doubts and worries about the future. This time with Dempsey was precious. A chance she'd been awaiting for half a lifetime.

Oh, what this man could do to her. With his hands. His sinful lips. The powerful thrust of his hips. He was better than any fantasy she'd dreamed up in the days when she'd had a crush on him.

"I was obsessed with this." Reaching behind her, he hooked a finger in the loop of the tie for her dress's halter top. "Do you have any idea how provocative it is to wear an outfit that allows a man to get you naked with a single tug on a lace?"

Her skin tightened like shrink-wrap.

"I hadn't known." Her neck tingled where his knuckles grazed it. "But now that I do, I will put the knowledge to work the next time I want you thinking about me."

Keeping his finger threaded through the loop, he didn't pull it free, but simply palmed her bare back and drew her closer.

"I'm thinking about you lately, no matter what you're wearing." He breathed the words in the hollow under her ear, right before he kissed her and then licked a trail across her most vulnerable places as he headed lower toward her shoulder.

The rasp of his jaw was a gentle abrasion on her skin, a sexy contrast to the wet heat of his lips and his tongue. She liked knowing that she was on his mind as much as he lingered in hers. Against all reason, she wanted to stay there.

"Are we alone in the house?" she asked, an idea coming to mind to help her stay in Dempsey's thoughts.

With only three more weeks of working as his assistant remaining, she wanted to fill his home with memories of her. Of them.

"Absolutely." He lifted his head from his task, eyes flaming with heat. "Why? Afraid of being an exhibitionist?" He tugged on the tie to the halter top of her dress.

"I'd prefer tonight to be for your eyes only," she admitted, clutching the dress to her breasts before it could fall. "And actually, the reason I wore this dress was just in case dinner by the pool turned into a pool party."

She let go of the fabric, and it fell away. She wore a simple strapless red bikini beneath.

If Dempsey was disappointed she wasn't naked under her clothes, he sure didn't show it. In fact, he stared at her body in a way that felt deliciously flattering.

"Damn." He whistled softly as he slid a finger beneath the tie in the center of the bandeau top. "You mean I could have been watching you cavort around the pool in this?"

"It's not too late for a swim." She backed up a step and then another. "We could head outside—" she clutched the knot between her breasts and tugged it "—and skinny-dip."

Dempsey made a strangled sound as he came after her. She pivoted on her toes and raced through the kitchen and toward the back door with the hottest man she'd ever met on her heels.

Sprinting through the rear of the house, she found one of the French doors leading out to the pool. Only the underwater light illuminated the surface, although the grounds were decorated with low-wattage bulbs around the trees and bushes. The pool was well hidden from any prying eyes on the other side of the lake, the landscaping planted to provide natural privacy.

Adelaide slipped off her shoes and jumped in wearing only her bikini bottoms. Dempsey surprised her by diving in a moment after her wearing...nothing.

Her breath caught as the low lights reflected off his impressive frame. Strong thighs. Powerful shoulders. A butt that had no business being so appealing. And then a splash engulfed her and she had no more time to admire the man swimming across the pool toward her.

She made a halfhearted effort to get away because, of course, she couldn't wait to be captured.

When she felt a hand wrap around her ankle and drag her back through the water she welcomed the heat of his touch.

"That's not skinny-dipping," he accused, seizing her hips and dragging her bikini bottoms off before she could protest.

He flung them onto the deck with a wet splash, then backed her against a wall in the shallow end. Despite the slight chill of the water, his body was like an inferno against hers. He wrapped her in his arms, warming her, his erection trapped against her belly as he kissed her deeply. Thoroughly.

She got so lost in him she didn't know how long they stayed there, hands gliding over slick skin, tongues tangling as they moved together. She watched, fascinated with the way their bodies looked beside one another, his muscles so impressive in the moonlight.

"I want you inside me." She shifted her hips to stroke him with one hand as she circled his waist with her leg. "Please."

"I don't have any protection out here," he said in her ear, nibbling her earlobe and driving her mad with need.

She bit her lip against the hunger, already so close to release. She could just let go and enjoy the sensations he could pull from her so easily with his talented hands. But she wanted to hold out for having him deep inside her.

"Let's go in," she pleaded, the hollow ache almost painful.

Dempsey lifted her into his arms and climbed the built-in stairs while water sluiced off them. He must look like Poseidon, rising from the depths, but she was too busy kissing him to see for herself. He paused near a deck box and withdrew two prewarmed towels, laying both of them on her as he carried her against his chest.

"I can walk." She pulled back as he edged sideways through the open French door. "You can let me down."

"And risk having you run?" He nipped her ear. "I already caught my prize. I'm not letting go now."

He bypassed the main staircase for the narrow steps up from a butler's kitchen, probably because the thick rubber treads provided traction when they were still dripping wet.

"You're crazy if you think I'd run now." She delved her fingers into his wet hair and brought his lips to hers. "I keep thinking that I must have been dreaming last night and that sex couldn't have been as incredible as I remember. I want to see for myself. Again."

"I like a challenge." He angled into his bedroom and fell onto the bed with her, taking her weight on him as they rolled. Together. "Why don't you keep track of how many times I make you scream my name tonight?"

She might have laughed or teased him about that, but his hand was already between her legs, the heel of his palm pressing where she needed him most.

Desire shot through her like a Roman candle, a bright burst that fired again and again. She clung to him, calling out his name just as he'd promised she would. It was only the beginning, she knew. She hadn't imagined how thoroughly Dempsey would dominate her world, her thoughts, her nights.

She had gladly given him her body. But as tender feelings crowded her chest for this man, Adelaide feared she was giving him much, much more.

Nine

Dempsey awoke to the scent of coffee just how he liked it, thick and strong. Still half-asleep, he reached for Adelaide, only to find her side of the bed cold.

Coming more awake, he realized she must be responsible for making the coffee. He would have to tell her that he would far rather wake up to her in his arms, but he did appreciate the gesture on a game day. It was still dark out, but he needed to get to the stadium for their home opener—a banner moment in a career-making season. He could feel it in his bones.

And damn, but he would have liked to share that good feeling with Adelaide.

Shoving out of bed, he shrugged on a clean T-shirt and boxers, thinking he could coax her back upstairs. Then again, the kitchen table would do just fine. Last night had been so wild. So unexpected. He picked up his pace to find her.

When he reached the kitchen, he found her making breakfast in his shirt, her legs bare and her hair restrained in a messy braid that rested on her shoulder. But as he got closer, he could tell something was off by the way she moved. She fried eggs at the stove, her movements jerky and fast.

"Everything okay?" he asked as he passed the walk-in pantry. He might have lost his ability to read her more subtle emotions, but he'd have to be blind not to correctly interpret anger.

"No." She pulled down two plates from a cupboard and slid the eggs onto them. "I got up early because of a notification on my phone. I keep alerts on various buzzwords in the media as they pertain to you and the team." She pointed toward the kitchen table. "Have a seat and check out the morning paper."

Worry stabbed him hard in the gut as he headed toward the table.

"Is Marcus back in trouble?" He'd sprung the kid from jail on good faith, offering him a job helping Evan with some work for the Brighter NOLA foundation. Dempsey needed extra hands for a renovation project on a building that would house a local recreation center for the kids.

"No. Not this week anyway." Her clipped response gave nothing away as she retrieved silverware and linen napkins from a sideboard near the breakfast bar.

"Hurricanes Coach Muzzles Stormy Girlfriends." He read the headline aloud from the social section's front page. "Old news, right? Did she offer anything different than the rumors that have been around for years—that I rely on confidentiality agreements for some of my personal relationships?"

Was this what had Adelaide so riled? They'd seen worse and weathered it in the past.

"No." She put his eggs down on the table and tugged out a chair to sit across from him. "But nice timing on a game day, isn't it?"

"Whoa." He reached for her, bracketing her shoulders with his hands. "What am I missing? Why is this so upsetting?"

"Why?" Adelaide's eyes widened. "Because for all she knows we really *are* getting married. And what kind of evil witch does that to someone who is newly engaged?"

She blinked fast, emotions swirling through her eyes quicker than he could register them.

"Someone selfish." He shrugged, still not sure he saw what the big deal was, although he knew better than to say as much. "Someone who doesn't give any thought to who she hurts to get her own way. I'll bet you any money she wants to tout a new contract or sponsor or has some kind of promotional angle—"

He let go of her to turn the paper toward him so he could read the story.

"She has a part in a new action-adventure film," Addy admitted. "She mentions it toward the end."

"You see? Self-centered and trying to scam off the Hurricanes' publicity when a lot of people are paying attention to the team." He kissed Adelaide's cheek and pulled her to him again, holding her close, savoring the feel of her wearing precious little under that T-shirt. "C'mon. Let's have this breakfast you made. It smells fantastic."

"It's just eggs," she grumbled. Then her lips curled upward a bit. "Although I did make use of the cayenne pepper, which is why you like the scent, you crazy Cajun."

She hadn't called him that in a long time. Memories of their past—her friendship and unswerving loyalty—stirred along with it. Reminding him he didn't want to hurt her. She'd made him breakfast long ago when there'd been no food at his place. Eggs were a cheap meal, and even though he had access to the most exotic foods in the world, there was nothing he'd rather share with her right now than the eggs she'd cooked for him herself.

Taking care of him.

"Some spice in life is a good thing." He tugged her back and kissed her harder, more comfortable thinking about the chemistry they shared than that other, deeper connection. "And speaking of which, last night was incredible."

"I had fun, too." She shot him a flirtatious look as she took her seat at the table. "I'm glad you're not upset about the article in the paper—even if I'm still steaming a little."

He flipped it over and shoved it away.

"Not at all." He tucked her chair in and then sat beside her. "Valentina is annoying but predictable. I'm only upset for you."

He took a few bites before he noticed Addy had gone quiet. Glancing up, he noticed her studying him.

"Is that a plus when you're dating?" she asked, carefully cutting a piece of her egg and sliding it onto her toast. "Predictability trumps selfish and annoying?"

And just like that, he stood alone in a minefield with no foreseeable path out.

"You must know that I've deliberately simplified my

personal life these past few years in order to focus on my career." He set down his fork, realizing he should have paid more attention to the nuances of this conversation.

It wasn't about the article in the paper. Or about a potential distraction for him on his season opener.

Adelaide was more than a *little* angry about Valentina.

"You want simple *and* predictable." She tapped the heavy band of her engagement ring on the table. "It's strange that you opted to stage a relationship with me right now since it's both complicated and unexpected."

Didn't she understand that she was nothing like other women he'd been with? He wouldn't trade this time with her for anything.

"But you're not like other women, Addy. I trust you not to turn our private affairs into a three-ring circus for your own ends." He wanted to salvage a good day. He wanted to get back to where they were yesterday, when they'd had dinner with family and then driven each other wild all night long.

"You trust me to keep this simple and be predictable, too." She shook her head, a smile that was the opposite of happy twisting her lips. She shot out of her chair. "Unbelievable how the Reynaud arrogance has no bounds."

"Wait a minute." He stood as well, scrambling to follow her, to understand how he'd hurt her when that was the last thing he'd intended.

"No." The word was sharp. A short warning that her emotions were seething close to the surface.

He could see it in her face. In her eyes.

"Addy, please. Let me explain."

"No." She shook her head, her braid unraveling as she moved, since she hadn't bothered to wrap a tie around the end. "I'm going to drive separately to the stadium. And when I get there, I will be an excellent assistant, as I've always been. I'll even keep the ring on my finger. But don't ask me to pretend with you, Dempsey. Not today."

For a moment, he felt stunned, as if she'd kicked him in the solar plexus.

"What do you mean? You can't end our agreement—"

"Please." She held a hand up to stop that line of discussion. "I'm not ending anything except this conversation. But I'm asking you—don't put me on the spot today, okay? I might not be as predictable as you'd like to think."

Members of the media rushed onto the field after the Hurricanes won 21–17 in their home opener against the defending Super Bowl champs. Adelaide watched from the sidelines, a rare spot for her, since her duties were more behind-the-scenes. But after her exchange with Dempsey over breakfast that morning, she had been reminded that in three more weeks, she would no longer have a role on the team. She might never have the chance to witness a game from this vantage point again.

Rap music blared from the speakers in the stands, adding to the celebratory mood. Fans whooped it up with one another. While some headed out to the parking lots to party or drive home, many hardcore followers remained in the stands, getting as close to the field as ushers would allow.

A photographer with a camera and a big plastic sound shield shuffled past her, his lens trained on Dempsey where he shook hands with the opposing team's coach. A coach who did not look happy. The guy's face was still red after a screaming match with a ref about a pass-interference call that had not happened.

But the Hurricanes' game one was in the books. Dempsey and his team were off to the start he'd wanted for this season, the start that meant so much to him. Logically, she understood why. He'd always felt like an outsider in the Reynaud family, working relentlessly to prove he belonged, that his father had not made a mistake in plucking him out of that crappy apartment down the street from hers.

Yet, she couldn't help but think that if St. Roch Avenue wasn't good enough for him, then she wasn't good enough for him either. He'd dated one beautiful woman after another for years, never looking at Adelaide twice until she tried to quit. Hearing his easy defense of Valentina this morning had brought that hurt to the surface. When Adelaide's time with Dempsey was through, he'd go right back to women who were simple, predictable and from a much different world than hers.

She had no illusions about his ability to move on. She'd seen him do that plenty of times. But she seriously doubted hers.

Heading for the door that led into the medical staff's offices and bypassed the locker-room area, Adelaide picked up her pace when she saw a female reporter charging toward her, a cameraman in tow. Seriously?

The press on the field were normally big-time sports reporters, not from the social pages.

"Adelaide!" the woman called. "Excuse—"

Arriving at the door, Adelaide hauled it open and

risked a glance back to see what had happened to her follower.

Henri Reynaud, the Hurricanes' quarterback and Dempsey's younger brother, had planted himself between Adelaide and the woman. Addy's heart fluttered a bit. Not that she thought Henri was Mr. Dreamy the way the rest of the female fans did. But because Dempsey's brothers had made her feel as though she mattered this week. Gervais by inviting her to dinner. Henri by running interference.

Seeing how she might have been accepted into their world made her chest ache for the things she wasn't going to have with Dempsey. She would be walking away from so much more than a job in three weeks. So why was she spending this window of time second-guessing herself—and Dempsey—every time she turned around? Why couldn't she just enjoy the moment?

Maybe she needed to stop worrying about the future. Starting tonight, she wasn't going to look beyond three weeks from now.

She would save up her memories of being the woman who got to be on his arm and in his bed. The memories of being part of a family. They wouldn't be enough, but if they were all she would ever have of him, she would make each moment count.

Dempsey drove the fastest street-legal BMW produced to date, but it didn't get him out of downtown any quicker after the game.

Had he ever felt so uneasy after a win?

He switched lanes to pass a slow-moving car, his G-Power M5 Beemer more than ready to launch into overdrive at the earliest opportunity. Too bad the ribbon

of brake lights ahead meant he only succeeded in hurtling headlong from one stop-and-go lane to the next.

He'd asked the public relations coordinator if she'd
seen Adelaide, but Carole didn't know where his fiancée
had gone after the game. Now he gave in and phoned
Evan. Hitting the speed-dial icon on the dashboard, he
listened to Evan's line ring via Bluetooth.

"Hey, Coach. What's up?" Evan had lost his roster
spot due to injury, but unlike most guys who'd been in
the league for any length of time, he hadn't been in a
hurry to rehab and look for a new team in the spring.
He understood well the hazards of being a player and
had been content to simply stick around the team.

Dempsey had asked him about returning to school
for sports medicine and coming aboard as a trainer, but
Evan called himself a "simple guy with simple needs,"
insisting he liked driving the Land Rover.

"Just checking to see if you're taking good care of
my future wife." The comment didn't roll off his tongue
the way he thought it would.

His wife.

The idea made his chest go tight and he wasn't quite
sure why.

"She's teaching me about the garment business at
the moment. Just a sec." Clearly holding his hand over
the phone, Evan spoke to someone else—Adelaide, pre-
sumably. But a man's voice came through in the background, too. Then Evan came back on the line. "We're
just finishing up a tour of a manufacturing facility. She's
hoping that with some customization it might work out
for producing her apparel line."

Her apparel line. Dempsey ground his teeth together,
biting back a retort.

Apparently he hadn't made any headway yet convincing her to stay with the Hurricanes—with him—for the rest of the season. But then, he'd spent all his time romancing her after being surprised by an attraction he hadn't accounted for.

He needed to get their relationship back on track.

"I'd like to surprise her with dinner," he improvised, although maybe that wasn't a bad idea. "Are you bringing her home soon?"

Dinner aside, he just wanted to know when he would see Adelaide. She hadn't picked up her phone or answered his text after the game.

But then, she obviously took her start-up business more seriously than him.

"Definitely," Evan returned. "I think she's finishing up her meeting with the Realtor now. We're about half an hour away."

"Good deal. Thanks." Disconnecting the call, Dempsey pulled into the driveway of his house.

The outdoor lights were on, along with a few indoor ones. He had everything on timers, and he'd increased the periods when the grounds were lit, wanting to make the place as hospitable as he could for Adelaide.

Had her decision to tour a manufacturing facility been made this morning, spurred by her frustration regarding Valentina? Or had Addy been quietly taking care of her own business concerns all week, in spite of their agreement that she'd devote her time to the Hurricanes?

To him. This upset him far more than it should have.

His phone rang after he'd parked the BMW and headed into the house. Juggling his keys in one hand, he didn't check the caller ID before he thumbed the answer switch.

"Reynaud." He didn't need team problems. He had enough personal ones, since Addy was giving him the runaround.

"Hey, bro." The voice of his youngest brother came through the airwaves. "Congrats on the win."

"You, too, Jean-Pierre. I saw you put up some hellacious stats today." Dempsey hadn't been able to watch any film highlights on the way home, since he'd had to drive himself, but he'd checked for updates on the other one o'clock games before he left the stadium.

"Perfect football weather in New York. The ball sailed right where I wanted it to all day." The youngest Reynaud was the starting quarterback for the New York Gladiators and currently the only member of the family who wasn't a part of the Hurricanes organization. "Tomorrow's practice is light. I could head down there afterward if you think we need a powwow about Gramps."

"That'd be good. I think it's going to take all four of us to figure out how to approach him." Dempsey stepped inside the house, which was too quiet without Adelaide there.

Already, all his best memories in this place were with her.

Undressing her in the foyer. Chasing her out to the pool. Carrying her up to his bed.

"He's getting worse?" Jean-Pierre asked, pulling Dempsey's thoughts away from Addy.

"He thought I was Dad at a fund-raiser event the other night. Implied I needed to be careful my wife didn't find out about the woman on my arm."

On the other end, Jean-Pierre let loose a string of soft curses.

"That sucks," he finally said, summing it up well. "I'll be off the practice field by noon. I can probably be at the house by four." A perk of being in New York was that private planes were plentiful. Jean-Pierre didn't come home often, but he could make the trip in a hurry when he needed to.

"Sounds good. We practice at noon, but I'll make sure we finish up in time. See you then." Disconnecting the call, he knew he'd have to go in early to meet with his assistant coaches and watch game film.

Hell, he'd be watching game film tonight, too. But first, he would order dinner for him and Adelaide. Do something nice for her to make up for all the things he'd said wrong over breakfast. Maybe then he would be able to confront her about that trip to see a potential manufacturing facility. The capital investment for a start-up business would compromise her operating costs. She had to know that.

Her role with the Hurricanes aside, it was too soon for her business to launch in that kind of direction. Small growth was wiser. Subcontracting the manufacturing would give her more cushion for expenditures. As much as he understood she didn't want him interfering with this company she wanted to build, he simply couldn't let her fail.

Ah, hell, who was he kidding? He might be a selfish bastard, but he couldn't ignore the truth.

He didn't want her to leave.

Ten

"No one could hold a grudge after that dinner." Adelaide swirled a strawberry through a warm chocolate sauce served in a melting pot over an open flame. "I might have to pick fights with you more often if this is the aftermath."

Dempsey had ordered an exquisite meal to be catered for them, and considering it must have been on short notice, the food was outrageously delicious. Her scallops had been prepared in a kind of sauce that took them from good to transcendent. The grilled vegetables were hot and tender, perfectly seasoned. But the dessert of exotic fondues was inspired.

She couldn't get enough of the chocolate sauce with a hint of raspberry liqueur.

"Are you sure?" Dempsey asked her, reaching under the mammoth dining room table to skim a touch along her knee. "I know you were upset this morning."

They were seated diagonally from one another—he was at the head of the table and she was to his right. The table was a chunky dark wood handcrafted in Mexico, the coarse finish making the piece all the more masculine and right for the house. Adelaide liked all the decor even if—in her fanciful imaginings—she pictured what she would do if she lived here. She'd put a vase of birds of paradise on the table, for one thing. Bright splashes of color to warm up this cool, controlled world.

"I was upset," she admitted. "But as I stood on the sidelines today, it occurred to me that I don't want to spoil this time with you. Working for you has been an incredible opportunity and I will miss it… I have to confess I will miss working with you, as well. Seeing you."

"Tell me what else you'll miss." He pulled her bare foot into his lap and massaged the arch.

"That feels amazing." She settled deeper into the red leather cushion on her high-backed wooden chair. Popping a raspberry into her mouth, she told herself she could have one more chocolate treat if she ate two plain berries.

Those were actually delicious as well, the juicy fruit almost tart after the sweetness of the chocolate.

"Turn your chair and I can do both feet." He nodded toward the side that needed shifting. And sure enough, pivoting toward him made it more comfortable to give him her other foot, too.

His thumbs stroked up the centers, over and over.

"What else will I miss?" She repeated the question to remind herself what he'd asked her before she slipped into a foot-massage-induced trance. "Always having a seat for the big games. The scent of barbecue in the

parking lot from the tailgaters before home games. Seeing the young players at training camp and watching
them horseplay because they're overgrown kids."

He was quiet for so long she wondered what he was
thinking.

But hadn't she promised herself to simply enjoy this
time with him? To make the most of every day of these
next few weeks?

"I'll bet chocolate sauce would taste good on you,"
she observed lightly, dragging the warm pot closer.

That captured Dempsey's attention completely. He
slowed the foot massage.

"The catering staff is still here," he reminded her,
peering over his shoulder toward the kitchen.

They hadn't seen anyone since dessert was brought
out, but two servers waited behind the scenes to clear
their dishes and put away the leftovers.

"I'll bet they won't mind billing you for a fondue pot
if I bring it upstairs with me."

Releasing her feet, he pushed back from the table in
a hurry. He took the sauce from her, securing it under
one arm, and then pulled out her chair to give her more
room to stand.

A gentleman.

"No." He put a hand on her back and guided her
away from the staircase. "Your room this time. You've
got that big tub for afterward, and I think we're going
to need it."

A thrill shot through her. Something about this new
pact she'd made with herself—to live in the moment and
store up these memories—made her bolder. More willing to take chances with him and see what happened.

He was already prepared to walk away from their

engagement in three more weeks, so why not at least ask for the things she wanted in a way she never had before? Chocolate sauce all over Dempsey… It was the stuff of fantasies.

Except once they closed the door to her bedroom, he set her decadent treat on the glass top of a double dresser, and then spun her in his arms. A whirlwind of raw masculinity, he hauled her up in his arms and carried her toward the large bathroom, his eyes blazing with undeniable heat.

"Dessert?" she asked, walking her fingers up his chest, her breathing unsteady at the feel of his arms around her.

"It's going to have to wait," he growled. "If you wanted slow and sweet, you shouldn't have looked at me like that over the dinner table."

A laugh burst free, but it turned into a moan as he settled her on the vanity countertop and stepped between her legs.

"I have no idea what you're talking about," she teased, her mouth going dry as he bunched up the fabric of her skirt and snapped the band on her panties with a quick tug.

Fire roared over her skin.

"The look you gave me?" He passed her a condom a second before he dropped his pants. "It said you wanted me right here." He slid a finger inside her.

The condom fell from her fingers. She wound her arms around his neck, needing more of him. All of him. Her heartbeat pounded so fiercely she felt light-headed. She pressed her breasts to his chest, doing her best to shrug out of the bodice. He must have retrieved the condom because she could feel the graze of his knuckles against her while he rolled it into place.

And then he was deep inside her.

His thrusts were hard, fast, and she loved every second of being with him. She held on tight, meeting his movements with her own as she caught glimpses of them moving together reflected in the mirrors all around. His powerful shoulders all but hid her from view from the back. But from the side, she saw her head thrown back, her spine arched to lift her breasts high. He ravished them thoroughly, one hand palming the back of her scalp while the other guided her hip to his.

Again and again.

"Let me watch you, Addy," he whispered in her ear, his breath harsh. "Come for me."

And she did.

Pleasure burst through her with fiery sparks, one after the other. He followed her, muscles flexing everywhere as he joined her in that hurtle over the edge.

His hand swept over her back, holding her close, his forehead falling against hers. She clutched at the fabric of his shirt, amazed that he was still half-dressed.

When she caught her breath, she pulled back, looking up at him. She wasn't sure what she expected—a smile, perhaps, for the crazy bathroom sink encounter. But she hadn't expected the seriousness in his eyes. Or the tenderness.

There was a connection there. A moment of recognition that sex hadn't been just about fun and pleasure. Something bigger was happening. She felt it, as much as she didn't want to. Did he?

Maybe he did. Because just then he blinked. But the

moment had passed. The look had vanished. His expression was now carefully shuttered.

She knew it would be wisest, safest, to pretend that moment had never happened. To keep things light and happy and work on stockpiling those memories before she left to start over—a new career, a new life.

But it took every ounce of willpower she possessed to simply call up a smile.

"Where did that come from?" She walked her hands down the front of his chest, admiring his strength.

His beautiful body.

"I missed you today," he said simply. "It didn't feel right, starting our day off arguing." He shifted positions and helped her down from the counter.

They cleaned up and she followed him into the bedroom. She sprawled on the California king–size mattress beside him, pulling pins out of her hair and setting them on the carved wood nightstand.

"Well, I sure don't feel like arguing after that amazing meal and the…rest." She laid her head on his chest and listened to his heartbeat.

In some ways, she would miss these moments even more than the torrid, tear-your-clothes-off encounters. A swell of emotions filled her, and she couldn't resist kissing the hard, muscular plane.

This, right now, was her best memory so far. Being cradled in his arms and breathing in the pine scent of his soap.

"All day it was on my mind, how much I wanted to get home and fix things with you." He stroked fingers through her hair.

That moment of connection in the bathroom? Could he feel it even now?

But she knew him well. Knew that he'd pushed away his other lovers once they started to get too close. Expect more from him. As his friend, she wouldn't follow that same path. There had to be some way to salvage at least their friendship when this was all over.

"I have the perfect stress reliever that will make you feel better about your day." She sat up on the bed, letting her hair fall over her shoulder now that she'd taken it all down.

Light spilled in from the bathroom, casting them in shadows. They'd eaten dinner late after the game and she knew he'd have to watch his game film soon.

"My stress faded as soon as I got you alone." His wicked grin made her heart do somersaults.

"Take off your shirt and turn over," she commanded, already plunging her fingers under the hem of his T-shirt.

"Yes, ma'am," he drawled, his eyes lighting with warmth again as he dragged the cotton up and over his head.

"You know how they say chocolate is good for the soul?" She retrieved the dessert sauce and dipped a finger in the warm liquid.

"I think it's books that are good for the soul." He propped his head on a pillow, his elbows out.

"Well, chocolate is good for mine." She traced the center of his spine with her finger, painting a line of deliciousness and then following it with her tongue. "But I think you're going to like this, too."

An hour later, she'd proved chocolate was good for everyone. Dempsey had bathed her afterward, whispering sweet words in her ear while he washed her hair.

She felt sated and boneless by the time he slipped

from her bed to put in the necessary hours at his job. She hated that he couldn't sleep with her all night, but in some ways, she wondered if it was for the best. She could tell herself that he had to work to do, and maybe that would make the hole he'd left in her heart a little more bearable.

Dempsey was still thinking about Adelaide the next day when he arrived at Gervais's house to meet with his brothers. Physically, he stood outside the downstairs media room and made himself a drink at the small liquor cabinet in the den. But mentally, his brain still played over and over the events of the night before.

Mostly, he thought back to that electric shock he'd felt when he'd looked into her eyes and the earth shifted. He couldn't write off that moment when he'd never experienced if before with any other woman. He had feelings for Adelaide. And that was going to complicate things in more ways than he could imagine.

"Dude." Jean-Pierre strode into the den behind him. "You're getting old when that passes for a drink. I come to town once in a blue moon. You can do better than—" he held up the bottle to read it "—coconut water? You'd better turn in your man card."

"I get the last laugh when I live longer." Dempsey set down his drink to give his brother a light punch in the stomach, a favored family greeting that their grandfather had started when they were kids.

Jean-Pierre returned with a one-two combination that—while still mostly for show—made Dempsey grateful he maintained a rigorous ab workout. Of all his brothers, he was closest to Jean-Pierre, making him the only one in the family he still punched.

"You'll be a hundred and five and wishing you'd had more fun in your life," Jean-Pierre joked, going straight for the scotch decanted into cut crystal. "I've got transportation home tonight, so I don't mind if I crack open the stash Gervais likes to hide at the back of the cabinet."

"You have no idea where I hide my real stash." Gervais stalked out of the media room, where game film seemed to run on a continuous loop during the regular season. "I leave the swill out when I know the hard drinkers are coming."

Gervais hugged their brother.

"Did someone say swill?" Henri ambled out of the media room, where he must have been already watching film with Gervais. "Sounds like my kind of night—as long as I don't have to drink with any holier-than-thou New York players."

Even as he said it, he one-arm hugged Jean-Pierre. The two of them were more competitive with the rest of the world than each other. It had always made Dempsey a little sick inside to see them go up against one another on the field, since he genuinely wanted both of them to win. They were incredibly gifted athletes who, in a league full of gifted athletes, walked on a whole different plane.

"Sit," Gervais ordered them. "You are busy and it's rare we're all together. I'd like to deal with the issue at hand first so we can relax over dinner."

"Relax?" Jean-Pierre lounged sideways in one of the big leather club chairs arranged around the fireplace in the den. "Who can relax while Gramps is struggling to remember his own grandsons?"

The mood shifted as they each gravitated toward the

spots they'd always taken in the room from the time they were kids and Theo would call them in for talks. Or, more often, when they had run of the house because their father was on an extended "business trip" that was code for a vacation with his latest woman.

When the house had still belonged to Theo and Alessandra, most of the rooms had been fussy and full of interior-decorator additions—elaborate crystal light fixtures that hung so low the brothers broke something every time they threw a ball in the house. Or three-dimensional wall art that spanned whole walls and would scrape the skin off an arm if they tackled and pushed each other into it.

The den had always been male terrain.

Now Dempsey got them up to speed on his exchange with Leon at the Brighter NOLA fund-raiser.

Silence followed, each one of them ruminating on the possibility that Leon was in the early stages of dementia.

"You do take after Dad the most," Henri offered from his seat behind the desk, Italian leather shoes planted on the old blotter. He lifted a finger from his glass to point at Dempsey.

His shoulders tensed. Every muscle group in his arms and back contracted.

"Henri," Gervais warned.

"Seriously, he looks more like Dad. He has his walk, too. Grand-père might have been—"

"I am nothing like our father." He had to loosen his hold on the cut-crystal glass before he shattered it.

He'd done everything to distance himself from Theo from the moment he'd arrived in this house as a teen. He could count the number of drinks he took in a year on one hand. As for women? He'd had contractual arrangements with every single one but Adelaide, and the time frames had never overlapped. There would never be a surprise child of his who would be raised alone. Separated from family.

"I know, man. But you've got the whole drama with the model going on the same week you get engaged. Maybe Leon just got a little muddled and—"

Dempsey was across the floor and knocking Henri's feet off the desk before the sentence was done.

"Not. The. Same." Fury heated the words.

"Seriously?" Henri put his drink down. "Are we going there? Because I'm not getting bounced off the team for some bullshit argument in the den, but if I have to pound you, I will."

Dempsey had more to say to that, since any pounding that needed doing would be meted out by him. But Gervais clapped him on the shoulder.

"Henri just doesn't want to face the fact that Leon isn't indestructible. Maybe give him a pass today." Gervais spoke calmly. Rationally.

And, probably, correctly.

No one wanted to think about their grandfather going downhill. They all loved the old man.

"I would never cut you for an argument in the den." Dempsey extended the olive branch. "But just so we're clear, I could still kick your ass."

"Not responding." Henri returned his feet to the desk. "So no one else thinks it could have been a momentary lapse for Leon? One mistake and he's an Alzheimer's patient?"

"It's not just one. There were signs this summer, too," Gervais reminded them. "He was going to see his doctor about it and he said it was a thyroid condition. If that's the case, he needs to get his meds checked. But at this point, we might need to consider the idea that he's not really taking care of himself."

Dempsey drained his water, trying to focus on the conversation and let go of the dig about his overlapping affairs. Not that Henri had worded it that way, but damn. He'd worked so hard to distance himself from his father's philandering ways. Did his brothers still see him as some kind of playboy type?

Clearly they had no idea how far gone he was over Adelaide. He couldn't even imagine letting her go at the end of their engagement. By now he wasn't even as concerned about replacing her as his assistant.

He couldn't replace her in his bed. Or if he was honest with himself, his heart. She made him laugh. She understood his lifestyle and the huge demands of his job. She even made it easier for him to be around his family. That dinner with Gervais and Erika had been one of the most stress-free times he'd ever had with one of his brothers as an adult, perhaps because he wasn't reading slights into the conversation the way he did today with Henri.

"Dempsey?" Jean-Pierre's voice knifed through his thoughts. "What do you think we should do?"

"Spend as much time with him as we can." It was all he knew how to do with people who weren't staying in his life forever. He knew it was a crap plan even as he proposed it, but he hadn't figured out anything better for keeping Addy around either.

Throughout the meal he shared with his brothers, he kept coming back to that point. He had no plan for convincing Adelaide to stay. He respected her for wanting to build her own business and he couldn't in good conscience prevent it from happening for his own selfish ends. He had to find a way to help her that would be an offer she couldn't refuse. A way to help her that wouldn't make her feel as if he was taking the power out of her hands.

He understood that much about her.

But their time shared as a newly engaged couple had shown him how good they could be together, and he refused to walk away from that without giving the relationship more time. Every day he couldn't wait to be with her. Even sitting around with his brothers in a rare meal where they were all in the same place, Dempsey was still picturing that moment when he would head home and see Addy.

She made sense in his life and she always had.

He would make a case for extending their engagement. No, damn it. He would propose to her for real. They had been friends. They'd worked together. He counted on her.

Now? Their chemistry was off the charts and they brought each other a level of fulfillment that he'd never experienced before. Adelaide was a smart woman. She would understand why they worked together.

She had to.

Eleven

"I think it's a great space, Adelaide." Her mother walked through the riverside manufacturing facility that Adelaide could use for mass-producing knitwear. Della's purple flip-flops slapped along the concrete floor.

"The square footage for offices is nice, too." She headed toward the back of the building to show her mother. Her Realtor had opened the door for them as long as Adelaide would lock up behind them.

She was already subcontracting out a short run of shirts after her success with crowd funding, but the time had come to think bigger. And this space would be ideal, already containing a few machines she would refit for the kind of textile production she needed. She'd been approved for a small-business loan that would cover the cost of the building and her biggest start-up expenses, but it was still a big step and she wanted her mother's opinion.

Lately, it felt as though her life was on fast-forward, and while it was exciting to have so many new options open to her, a part of her wished she could just stop for a minute and be sure she was making the best decisions. Dempsey jumbled all her thoughts lately, the passion they shared so much different from her old crush. She wasn't sure if she trusted herself to move forward in any direction.

"What does Dempsey think about it?" Della asked, examining the floor-to-ceiling windows overlooking the Mississippi in the largest of the offices.

"He hasn't seen it yet." She hated to admit as much, but he'd been so dismissive of her dreams before, so ready to leap in and save her from her own mistakes, that she wasn't ready to share this with him.

Then again, maybe moving ahead with her business simply signaled an end to her time as Dempsey's fiancée and she wasn't sure if she was ready for it to be over.

Della's brows arched. "Too busy to make time for my girl's work?"

"No. Nothing like that." She closed her eyes, hating the lies. And would it really matter if she told her mother the truth? Della Thibodeaux didn't exactly have a history of running to the press with gossip. "He didn't want me to tell anyone, but the engagement is just for show. I did it to help him."

Or because he'd put her in a ridiculously awkward position, take your pick.

But she couldn't regret it after how close they'd grown. The only problem was, now that she'd seen how amazing it was to be with him—even better than she'd ever imagined—she had no idea how she'd ever go back to their old friendship.

"Just for show?" Della folded her arms, leaning into the window frame as she studied her daughter, deep concern in her eyes.

Sunlight spilled in all around her, catching the grays in her dark hair. Her mother was a beautiful woman and so wise, too. Addy couldn't deny being curious to hear her mother's opinion on the fake engagement. Would she tell Adelaide she was the most foolish woman ever?

"He announced it in public and made it difficult for me to argue it without humiliating him."

"Of course you didn't argue, because you've always wanted to make him happy." She strode closer and put her hands on Adelaide's shoulders, her heavy silver bracelets settling against Adelaide's collarbone. "And is it still for show now, after you've been living with him for almost two weeks?"

Her cheeks heated, which was silly because she was a grown-up and could live with whomever she wanted.

"I think I'm in love with him," she admitted, the words torn from her heart, since she knew that level of emotion was not reciprocated.

"Oh, sweetheart." Her mother opened her arms, gathered her close and squeezed tight. "Of course you do. At least one of you has admitted it."

Adelaide's eyes burned. Tears fell as she rested her head on her mother's shoulder. She didn't want her mother's pity for loving a man who didn't—

Wait. She stopped crying, her mother's words sinking in.

"What did you say?" Her thoughts caught up with her ears and she pulled back to look into her mom's hazel eyes, which were lighter than Adelaide's.

"You heard me." Della kissed her cheek and stepped

back. "You two were meant to be. You just needed the right time to come along. Why do you think he's thirty-one years old and dating fluff-headed women with more boobs than brains?"

Adelaide choked on a much-needed laugh. "Mom. That's not fair."

Even if, in her meaner moments, Adelaide might have been equally unkind in her thoughts. Mostly about Valentina.

"All I mean, daughter dear, is that he has never dated a woman seriously. I think it's because he's been waiting for the right woman. He's been waiting for you, my girl." She looped her arm around Adelaide's waist as they headed for the exit and shut off the lights.

Adelaide's yellow-diamond engagement ring caught the sun's rays, sending sparkles in every direction.

"That's such a mom thing to say." Still, it warmed her heart even if she knew Dempsey far better than her mother. "Does parenting come with a handbook of mom sayings to cheer up dejected daughters?"

She wanted to trust in her mother's words but she was scared to believe that Dempsey could care about her like that.

"Mothers know." She tipped her temple to Addy's, the scent of lemon verbena drifting up from her hair.

"Well, I'm not sure about the engagement or where that's going, but I'll tell him about this manufacturing space tonight. The Hurricanes play in Atlanta tomorrow and I'm going with him. After the game, we'll have some time together to talk and I'll see what he thinks." Or she hoped they would have time together.

Last Sunday, after their home opener, they'd had a nice dinner. But Dempsey had seemed distracted this week, ever since his dinner with his brothers. She knew he was worried about his grandfather, but it seemed as if he'd been busy every night since, only falling into bed with her at midnight and sleeping for a few hours.

He also made hot, toe-curling love to her until she couldn't see straight. She couldn't complain about that part. But she did wish she had more time with him, since it felt as though the clock was ticking down on their arrangement.

And no matter what her mother said to cheer her, Adelaide had seen no sign from Dempsey that he'd fallen in love.

"I'm dying to know where you're taking me." Adelaide glanced over at Dempsey sitting beside her in the limo he'd booked after the game. "I've never known you to be so mysterious."

When she'd checked into the hotel where the team was staying the night before, the concierge had given her a card from Dempsey, who had on-site duties at the Atlanta stadium when they'd landed. The card had invited her on a date to an undisclosed location after Sunday's one-o'clock game against Atlanta. A jaw-dropping Versace gown awaited her in their suite, burgundy lace with a plunging neckline that kept everything covered but—wow. The Louboutin sky-high heels that accompanied it were the most exotic footwear she'd ever slid on, the signature red sole dazzling her almost as much as the satin toes with hand-crafted embellishments.

If she looked down her crossed legs now, she could see the pretty toes peeping out from the handkerchief hem of the tulle skirting.

He folded her hand in his, the crisp white collar of his

shirt emphasizing his deep tan gained from spending every day on the practice field. "I owed you a date night. You were kind enough to be my date for the Brighter NOLA ball, so it seemed like you ought to have a night that was just for you."

His Tom Ford tuxedo was obviously custom tailored, since off-the-rack sizes never fit an athlete's body, and the black fabric skimmed his physique perfectly. The black silk-peaked lapels made her itch to run her hand up and down the material.

Later.

For now she just wanted to know where they were headed. She'd never seen Dempsey race out of a stadium so early. She hadn't even attended the game, taking her time to dress in the hotel, then taking the limo to the VIP pickup outside the stadium. Traffic had been slow at first, but it wasn't even six o'clock yet. Almost two hours before sunset.

"I'd be surprised if there are many restaurants out this way," she observed, peering out the windows as they drove toward Stone Mountain, winding through quieter roads.

It was early yet, but her invitation had mentioned a special "sunset dinner."

A mysterious smile played around his mouth. A mouth that had brought her such pleasure.

"There's a surprise first. I hope you're not too hungry."

"I think I'm too excited to be hungry." She felt the first flutter of nerves, because Dempsey looked so serious for a date night.

She wanted to ask him about that. About his grandfather's health. Maybe that was what had been bothering him all week. But just then, the limo came to a clearing in the trees and a flash of rainbow-colored silk fluttered through the sky.

"How beautiful!" She clutched his arm, pointing to a hot-air balloon being inflated on a nearby field.

At the same moment, the limo slowed and turned into the field, heading right toward the balloon.

She stilled.

"Don't tell me..." She turned toward him, and saw the first hint of a smile on his face. "Is this the surprise?"

"Only if you'd like it to be." He squeezed her hand.

She squealed, scarcely able to take her eyes off the huge balloon that looked as if it would burst into flames any moment from the blazing blasts that shot into the bottom, filling it with air. Or helium. Or whatever did that magic trick that made it go from half on the ground to a big ball in the sky.

"Yes!" She risked her lipstick by kissing him through a shocked laugh. "It's amazing! I've never seen anything like it."

"Here." He produced a satin drawstring bag as the car rolled to a stop and their driver came around to open the door. "Better wear these for now and save your pretty shoes for later."

Opening the sack, she pulled out a pair of silver ballet slippers. Just her size.

"You thought of everything." She had to have him help her because she fumbled the shoes twice, distracted by the sight of yellow, blue, red and orange silk rising higher just outside the car.

"I would have tried to get us here earlier if I'd known you wanted to see this part." His warm hands tugged her shoes into place before he helped her out of the car. He reached back in the limo and withdrew a length of fuzzy mohair and cashmere that at first she thought was a blanket, but he unfurled it and laid it around her shoulders. A burgundy-colored pashmina fell around her. "The pilot said it will be cooler once we're up there."

A red carpet lined her path from the car door to the balloon basket. While the limo driver exchanged words with the crew that operated the balloon, Adelaide had a moment to catch her breath and take in the full extent of her surprise. Blasts of heat passed her shoulders in rhythmic waves each time the pilot pulled the cord to unleash flames into the air that kept the balloon filled.

"I just can't believe how huge it is up close." She'd seen hot-air balloons in the sky before and admired their beauty, but she'd never dreamed of riding in one. "And I can't imagine what made you think to do this tonight, but I'm so excited I feel…breathless."

He tucked her close to his side as they walked the carpeted path together. "The best part hasn't started. I hear it's incredible to go up in one of these things."

"You've never done this either?" That made it feel all the more special, that she could share a first with him. She felt like a medieval princess, traipsing through the countryside in her designer gown, the layers of handkerchief hem blowing gently against her calves as they walked.

"No. This is just for you, Adelaide." He stopped as they reached the balloon basket, his eyes serious. Intense.

"Any special occasion?" Curious, she wasn't sure why he'd put so much effort into a special night for them now.

As much as she wanted to believe that he'd planned a fairy-tale date just to romance her, a cynical part of her couldn't help but wonder why.

"I'm sorry I put you on the spot when I announced our engagement. Consider this my apology, since that's not how I should have treated a friend." He lifted her hand to his lips and kissed the back of it.

Her heart melted. Just turned to gooey mush. She would have swooned into his arms if the pilot hadn't turned to them right then and introduced himself.

While the pilot—Jim—went over a few safety precautions and briefly outlined the plan for their hour-long flight, Adelaide stared at Dempsey and felt herself falling faster. She'd tried to keep herself so safe with him, from him. But her mother was right, and this man had always had a piece of her heart. How on earth could she maintain her defenses around a man who bought her a Versace gown to take her on a hot-air balloon ride?

She hadn't heard any of Jim's speech by the time Dempsey lifted Adelaide in his arms and set her on her feet inside the basket. He vaulted in behind her, their portion of the basket separated from Jim's by a waist-high wall. Moments later, the ground crew let go of their tethers and the balloon lifted them into the air so smoothly and silently it felt like magic.

Her heart soared along with the rest of her.

Impulsively, she slid her arms around Dempsey's waist and tucked her head against his shoulder. He'd said he wanted to apologize for not being a better friend. Could that mean he wanted to be...more?

"Do you like it?" His hand gripped her shoulder through the pashmina, a warm weight connecting them. They stared out their side of the basket while Jim took care of maneuvering the balloon from his own side. It felt private enough, especially with all the open air around them.

"I love it." She peered up at him as the world fell away beneath them. "I've never had anyone do something so special for me."

"Good." He kissed her temple while the limo below them became a toy-size plaything. "Because the past two weeks have been something special for me. I wanted you to know that, even if this engagement got off to an awkward beginning, it's been...eye-opening."

She reached for the edge of the basket and gripped it, feeling as though she needed an anchor in a world suddenly off-kilter. What was he saying? Had her mother guessed correctly that Dempsey cared more than she'd realized?

"How so?" Her voice was a thin crack of sound in the cool air, and she tugged the pashmina closer around her. The landscape spread out below them like a patchwork quilt of green squares dotted with gray rocky patches and splashes of blue.

"We make a great team, for one thing." He turned her toward him, his hands on her shoulders. "You have to know that. And you've spent years helping me to be more successful, always giving me far more help than what I could ever pay you for. I want you to know that teamwork goes both ways, and I can help you, too."

He withdrew a piece of paper from the breast pocket of his tuxedo. It fluttered a little in the breeze as the temperature cooled.

"What is it?" She didn't take it, afraid it would blow away.

"The deed to the manufacturing facility you looked

at with Evan last week." He tucked the paper into her beaded satin purse that sat on the floor of the balloon basket and straightened.

"You bought it?" She wasn't sure what to say, since she'd told him she didn't want this to be a Reynaud enterprise. "You haven't even seen it. I was going to ask you what you thought when we got back home—"

"I toured it Thursday before practice. It's a good investment."

The balloon dipped, jarring her, but no more than his words.

He'd toured it and bought it without speaking to her. She didn't want to ruin their balloon ride by complaining about what he'd obviously meant as a generous gesture. But she couldn't help the frustration bubbling up that he hadn't at least spoken to her about it.

"I hadn't even run the numbers on the operating costs yet." She didn't want to feel tears burning the backs of her eyes. She understood him well enough to know his heart was in the right place. But how could he be friends with her for so long and not understand how important it was for her to make her own decisions regarding her business? "I hadn't decided for sure yet—"

"You showed me the business plan, remember? I ran the numbers. You can afford the expenses easily now."

Except she needed to make those decisions, not him. Didn't he have any faith in her business judgment?

"Perhaps." She watched an eagle soaring nearby, the sight so incredible, but more difficult to enjoy when her world felt as if it was fracturing. "But I can't accept a gift—"

"I know you don't want anything handed to you, Addy, but this is no more of a gift than all the ways you've anticipated my every need for years. How many times have you worked more than forty hours in a week without compensation?"

"I'm a salaried employee," she reminded him, still feeling off balance.

"In a job that you took to help me. Don't try to make the deed mean more than it does, Adelaide. You've worked hard for me and I'm finally in a position to achieve everything I've always wanted with the Hurricanes this year. Let me be a small part of your dream, too."

Some of her defensiveness eased. She had to admit, it was a thoughtful gesture. A generous one, too, even if a bit high-handed. And the way he'd worded it made her feel a teeny bit more entitled to the gift, even though it far surpassed the monetary value of what she'd done for him. Still, the gift left her feeling a little hollow inside when she'd just convinced herself that he'd taken her on a balloon ride because he'd realized some deeper affection for her.

"Can I think about it before I accept it?" She cleared her throat, trying not to reveal the letdown she felt. The wind whipped a piece of her hair free from her updo, the long strand twining around her neck.

"No. You can sell it if you don't want to use the facility. But it's yours, Addy. That's done." He reached to sweep aside the hair and tucked it into one of the tiny rhinestone butterflies that held spare strands. "I have one other gift for you, and I want you to really consider it."

That seriousness in his eyes again. The look that had made her nervous all week. What on earth was on the man's mind?

When he reached into his breast pocket again, her heart about stopped. He pulled out a ring box.

Her heartbeat stuttered. Her gaze flew back to his.

"Adelaide, these two weeks have shown me how perfect we are together." He opened the box to reveal a stunningly rare blue garnet set in…of all things…a tiny spoon ring design that replicated the spoon bracelet he'd given her all those years ago when he'd had to forge a gift for her with his own hands.

"Dempsey?" Her fingers trembled as she reached to touch it, hardly daring to believe what she was seeing. What she was hearing.

"It's not meant to replace your engagement ring. But I wanted to give you something special."

"I don't understand." She shook her head, overwhelmed by the generosity of the gift.

"We're best friends. We're even better lovers. And we're stronger together." He tugged the ring from the velvet backing for her and slid the box into his pocket. "This ring is my way of asking you to make our engagement a real one. Will you marry me?"

Her emotions tumbled over each other: hope, joy, love and— Wait. Had he even mentioned that part? Of course he must have. She just hadn't heard it in the same way she'd missed the pilot's preliftoff speech because she'd been marveling at how perfect a date this was. She hadn't been paying attention.

Her hands hovered beside the ring.

"Did you…?" She felt embarrassed. Flustered. She should leap into his arms and say yes. Any other woman would. But Adelaide had waited most of her life to hear those words and she didn't want to miss any of it. "I'm sorry. I was so mesmerized by the ring and the setting and—" She gestured to the balloon above them and the scenery below. "It's all so overwhelming. But are you saying you want to get married? For real?" Happy tears pooled in her eyes already. "I love you so much."

And then she did fling herself into his arms, tears spilling onto the beautiful silk collar of his tuxedo. But she was just so happy.

Only…he still hadn't said he loved her. Her declaration of love hung suspended like a balloon between them. In fact, Dempsey patted her back awkwardly now, as if that was his reply.

She hadn't missed the words in his proposal, she realized with a heart sinking like lead. He simply hadn't said them. She knew, even before she edged back and saw the expression on his face. Not bewildered, exactly. More…unsure.

It wasn't an expression she'd seen on his face in many years. Her Reynaud fiancé was used to getting what he wanted, and while he might want Adelaide for a bride, it wasn't for the same reason that she would have liked to be his wife.

"Adelaide. Think about the future we can have together. All the things we can achieve." He must have seen her expression shifting from joy to whatever it was she was feeling now.

Deflation.

"Marriage isn't about being a team or working well together." She wrapped a hand around one of the ropes tying the basket to the balloon, needing something to steady her without the solid strength of Dempsey Reynaud beside her.

"There are far more reasons than that."

"There's only one reason that I would marry. Just one." She stared out at the world coming closer to them now. Dempsey must have signaled Jim to take them back down.

Their date was over.

"The ring is one of a kind, Adelaide. Like you." His words reminded her of all she was giving up. All she would be turning her back on if she refused him now.

But she'd waited too long for love to accept half measures now. She owed herself better.

"We both deserve to be loved," she told him softly, not able to meet his gaze and feel the raw connection that was still mostly one-sided. "You're my friend, Dempsey. And I want that for you as much as I want it for me."

When the balloon touched down, it jarred her. Sent her tumbling into his arms before the basket righted itself.

She didn't linger there, though.

Her fairy tale had come to an end.

Twelve

Three days later, back home at the Hurricanes' training facility, Dempsey envied the guys on the practice field. After the knife in the gut that had been Adelaide's rejection, he would trade his job for the chance to pull on shoulder pads and hit the living hell out of a practice dummy. Or to pound out the frustration through his feet with wind sprints—one set after another.

Instead, he roamed the steaming-hot practice field and nitpicked performances while sweat beaded on his forehead. He blew his whistle a lot and made everyone else work their asses off. Fair or not, teams were built through sweat, and he'd played on enough teams himself to know you balanced the good times—the wins—with the challenges. And if the challenges didn't come on the field on Sunday, a good coach handed them up in practice.

"Again!" he barked at the receivers running long patterns in the heat. Normally, Dempsey focused on the full team as they practiced plays. But today he had taken over the receiver coach's job.

In a minute, he'd move on to the running backs, since he'd already been through all the defensive positions.

Adelaide had not publicly broken their engagement yet, but she had moved out of his house. Which shouldn't have surprised him after the epic fail of his proposal. He'd planned for the moment all week. Spent every spare second that he wasn't with his team figuring out how to make the night special. Yet it had fallen short of the mark for her.

Of course, they hadn't gotten to half of it. He'd ordered an outdoor dinner set up in the mountains with a perfect view of the sunset. He'd had a classical guitarist in place, for crying out loud, so they could dance under the stars.

And she hadn't even taken her ring.

Of all the things that had gone wrong that night, that bothered him the most, given how much thought he'd put into the design. Sure, he was to blame for not understanding that he could have scrapped the balloon, the limo and the guitarist to simply say, "I love you." Except, in all his planning, that had never occurred to him. He'd known what he felt for Addy was big. But was it love? He'd shut down that emotional part of himself long ago, probably on one of the nights his mother had locked him out of the house, claiming some irrational fault on his part, but mostly because she was high.

Love wasn't part of his vernacular.

That had worked out fine for him in the Reynaud house full of men. Caring was demonstrated through externals. A one-two punch for a greeting like what he and Jean-Pierre still exchanged. Covering up for Henri when his younger brother had broken a priceless antique. His first well-executed corporate raid had won the admiration of Gervais and Leon alike.

Dempsey understood that world. It was his world, and he'd handed it to Adelaide on a silver platter, but it hadn't been enough.

And now he'd lost her in every way possible. As his friend. His lover. His future wife.

Stalking away from the receivers, he was about to put the running backs to work when his brother Henri jogged over to match his steps.

"Got a second, Coach?" Henri used the deferential speech of a player, a sign of respect Dempsey had never had to ask for, but which had always been freely given even though Henri thought nothing of busting his chops off the field.

"I probably have one." He kept walking.

Henri kept pace.

"Privately?" he urged in a tone that bordered on less deferential. "Practice was supposed to end an hour ago."

Surprised, Dempsey checked his watch.

"Shit. Fine." He blew his whistle loud enough for the whole field to hear. "Thanks for the hard work today. Same time tomorrow."

A chorus of relieved groans echoed across the field. Dempsey changed course toward the offices. Henri still kept pace.

"You're killing the guys," Henri observed, his helmet tucked under one arm, his practice jersey drenched with sweat. "Any particular reason?"

They were back to being brothers now that practice was done and no one would overhear.

"We have a tough game on Sunday and our first two wins have not been as decisive as I would have liked." He halted his steps and folded his arms, waiting for Henri to spit out whatever was on his mind. "You have a problem with that?"

"I'm all about team building." Henri planted a cleat on the first row of bleachers. "But you've run them long every day this week. Morale is low. The guys are confused in the locker room. I know that's not what you're going for."

"Since when do you snitch on locker-room talk about me?" Dempsey shooed away one of the field personnel who came by to pick up a water cooler. He didn't need an audience for this talk.

"Only since you started acting like a coach with a chip on his shoulder instead of the supremely capable leader you've been the whole rest of my tenure with this team."

The rare compliment surprised him. The complaint really didn't. There was a chance Henri was correct.

"I'll take that under advisement." He accepted the input with a nod and tucked his clipboard under one arm to head inside.

"So where's Adelaide?" Henri asked, stopping Dempsey in his tracks.

"Running her own business. Having a life outside the Hurricanes." Without him.

The knowledge still gutted him.

"Since I'm on a real roll with advice today, can I offer a second piece?" Henri brushed some dirt off his helmet.

"Definitely not." Pivoting away from his brother, he noticed some of his players were lying on the field.

Were they that tired? Had he run them that hard?

The idea bothered him. A lot.

"Dude, I'm not claiming to be an expert on women." Henri hovered at his shoulder, carrying the water cooler inside. "Far from it with the way my marriage is going these days."

The dark tone in Henri's voice revealed a truth the guy had probably tried hard to keep quiet.

"Sorry to hear it." Because even though Dempsey was waist high in self-pity right now, he felt bad for his brother.

"My point is, I know enough about women to know you're going about it all wrong."

"Tell me something I don't know."

Henri laughed, a loud, abrupt cackle. "How much time do you have, old man?" Then, tossing his helmet and the water cooler on the ground, he pantomimed a quick right hook to Dempsey's gut. "Seriously. Don't let Adelaide go."

And then he was gone, scooping up the helmet and shouldering the cooler to go hassle the slackers left on the field. No doubt reinstalling the team morale that Dempsey had single-handedly shredded.

He wasn't sure what had shocked him more. He'd never been particularly close with Henri, sensing that the guy had resented Dempsey more than the others as kids because Henri had been close with their mother. The mother who'd left as soon as Dempsey had set foot in the Reynaud house. But that was a long time ago, and maybe he needed to shake off the idea that he was a black sheep brother. Figure out how to be a better brother.

How to show he cared about people beyond stilted words about being good teammates.

Henri was right. It was time for Dempsey to stop expecting Adelaide to read between the lines with him. Just because she understood him better than anyone didn't excuse him from spelling out his feelings for her. She deserved that and much, much more.

So damn much more.

But he was going to lay it on the line for her again, without any distractions or big gestures. And hope like hell he got it right this time. Because the truth of the matter was he couldn't live without her. His championship season didn't mean anything if he couldn't share it with her.

The woman he loved.

Adelaide dug to the bottom of her pint of strawberry gelato while seated on her kitchen counter in the middle of the afternoon, wishing strawberry tasted half as good as chocolate ice cream.

Except everything chocolate reminded her of Dempsey after their chocolate-sauce encounter, and if she thought about Dempsey, she would cry. And after three days back home alone in her crappy apartment, she did not feel like crying anymore.

Okay, she did a little. Especially if she thought about how much effort he'd put into romancing her on Sunday after the game. How many other women would trade anything to be treated the way Dempsey treated her? Yet she'd discounted all his efforts in the hope of hearing he loved her.

Dumb. Dumb. Dumb.

Except that she'd do it all over again because she was

one of those romantic girls who believed the right guy would hand her his whole heart forever and ever. She didn't think she could go through life if that turned out to be a myth. Then again, she wasn't sure she could go another day without Dempsey.

But she could probably go through a few more single-serving-size gelatos. She'd bought every flavor that didn't contain chocolate, determined to find some new taste to love.

Her doorbell rang as she was on her way back to the freezer.

No doubt her mother on a mission of mercy to lift her spirits. Little did Della know that Adelaide was only going to stuff her with gelato to avoid hearing any kind platitudes about waiting for the right one to come along.

She yanked open the door, only to have the safety chain catch, and remembered too late she was supposed to look through the peephole. She didn't live in Dempsey's ultrasafe mansion anymore.

He stood on her welcome mat.

The man who hadn't left her thoughts in days wore black running shorts and a black-and-gold Hurricanes sideline T-shirt like the ones the players wore. He must have come straight from practice, because he made a point not to wander around town in team gear that made him all the more recognizable. He looked good enough to eat, reminding her why all the gelato in the world was not going to satisfy her craving.

"May I come in?" he asked, making her realize she'd stood there gawking without saying anything.

"Of course. Just a sec." She closed the door partway to remove the chain, then opened it again, more than a little wary.

She told herself it was just as well he'd stopped by, since she had wanted to give him that damn deed back to the manufacturing facility. Except he looked as tired as she felt, the circles under his eyes even darker than the ones she knew were on her face. The rest of him looked as good as ever, however, his thighs so deliciously delineated as he walked that she thought about all the times she'd seen them naked. Against her own.

"How'd practice go?" Her voice was dry and she cleared it. She'd continued to work for the team from home, not wanting to leave him in the lurch.

He hadn't said anything about her absence at the training facility, acknowledging her work-related emails with curt "thanks" that had been typical of him long before now.

"Poorly. I haven't been myself this week and I've been pushing the guys too hard. Henri called me on it today. I'm going to do better." He wandered around her living room, touching her things, looking at her paintings over the ancient nonfunctional fireplace.

She was surprised that he'd admitted to screwing up. No, that wasn't true. She was more surprised that he'd screwed up in the first place. He normally put so much effort into thinking how to best coach a team, he didn't make the type of mistakes he had described.

"I'm glad. That you're going to be better with the team, that is." Nervous, she wandered over to the refrigerator that was so old that modern retro styles copied the design. "Would you like a gelato?"

She pulled out a coconut-lime flavor and cracked open the top.

"No, thank you." He set down a statue of a cat that she used to display Mardi Gras beads. "I came here to bring you this. You left it behind when you moved out your things."

He set a familiar ring box on the breakfast bar dividing the living area from the kitchen. Her on one side. Him on the other. A ring in between.

As if her heart wasn't battered enough already.

"That stone is worth a fortune." She hadn't taken the yellow diamond either, of course. That one, she'd left on his bathroom vanity.

"And you're worth everything to me, so you can see you are well suited." He opened the box and took out the ring. "It's not an engagement ring. I'd already given you one of those. Adelaide, this one is the grown-up version of that bracelet I made you. Something you've worn every day of your life since I gave it to you."

"Friendship is forever," she reminded him, something he'd told her the day he gave it to her.

He came into the kitchen and eased her grip on the coconut-lime gelato, then set it on the linoleum countertop.

"I'm glad you remember that." He held the ring close to her bracelet. "Look and see how the patterns match."

"I see." She blinked hard, not sure what he was getting at. But she couldn't wear that beautiful ring on her finger every day without her heart breaking more.

"The spoon part is supposed to remind you that you're still my best friend. Forever." He slipped his hand around hers. "The rare blue garnet is there to tell you how rare it is to find love and friendship in the same place. And how beautiful it is when it happens."

Her gaze flipped up to his as she tried to gauge his expression. To gauge his heart.

"That's not what you said when you gave it to me."

She shook her head. "It's not fair to say things you don't mean—"

"I do, Adelaide." He took both her hands in his. Squeezed. "Please let me try to explain. I got it all wrong before, I know. But it was not for lack of effort."

"It was a beautiful date," she acknowledged, knowing she'd never recover from loving him. There would never be a man in her life like this one.

And it broke her heart into tiny pieces if he thought he could win her back by trotting out the right phrases.

"I spent so much time thinking about how to make the proposal perfect—how to make you stay—I never gave any thought to what *you* might want. What was important to *you*." He shook his head. "It's like spending all my time shoring up the defense and ignoring the fact that I had no offense."

She tried not to mind the sports metaphor. And, heaven help her, she did understand exactly what he meant.

"So I was just caught off guard at how much I missed the mark that day. It must tell you something that a mention of love threw me so far off my game I didn't even know what to say in return."

"You would know what to say if you felt it, too." She stepped back, needing to protect herself from the hurt this conversation was inevitably going to bring.

"No. Just the opposite. I didn't understand what I felt because I don't say those words, Addy." He looked at her as if he was perfectly serious.

And beneath the trappings of the wealthy, powerful man who was the CEO of international companies and would one day coach a team to the Super Bowl, Adelaide saw the wounded gaze of her old friend. The boy who hadn't been given enough love as a child yet still found enough kindness in his heart to rescue a little girl from a trouncing because he was an innately fair and honorable person.

He blinked and the look vanished as though it had never been, but she was left with an understanding that should have been there all along. She, who thought she knew him so well, hadn't seen the most obvious answer.

Dempsey Reynaud had never been in love. Had probably never spoken the words in his life to anyone. There was certainly never a mention of love in those notes she'd written to accompany the parting gifts to his old girlfriends.

"I understand." She nodded, the full weight of his explanation settling on her, yet still not quelling her concerns about the future, the ache of her heart. "But you can see why I'd want to feel loved and to hear that I'm loved if I was going to be your wife?"

She edged closer to him again, understanding now that she didn't need to worry about protecting her heart. If anything, she ought to think about his.

"I understand now. But it took three days of hell—not sleeping, not eating, missing you every second and damn near killing every guy on a fifty-three-man roster—to get it through my head." He swallowed hard. Tipped his forehead to hers. "So please, Adelaide, let me slide this ring on your right hand. And I want you to wear it forever because our friendship is even more beautiful now than when I gave you that bracelet so long ago."

She took a moment to think, to look in his eyes and see the truth. That they were bound together through years of love and friendship, tied together in a way that was strong. Lasting.

"Yes." She nodded. Kissed his rough cheek and liked it so much she kissed the other one, too. "But it's going to be hard being just friends after—"

He produced the second ring.

She made an unintelligible sound that might have been a cry of relief, hope or pure joy. She wasn't sure. She could feel her legs going unsteady beneath her, though.

"I brought this back with me, too." He held it between them, their foreheads still tipped together.

"It hurt leaving it behind." A few of her tears splashed down on it.

"It tore my heart from my chest to find it." He leaned back to kiss her forehead. Her temples. "But since I didn't get to personally put it on your finger the first time, I'm looking at this as my chance to do something right."

He got down on one knee in her tiny, ancient kitchen, his handsome face so intent on her that her heart did backflips.

"Adelaide Thibodeaux," he continued. "You are my heart and I am not whole without you. I love you more than anything. Will you do me the honor of being my wife?"

Speechless because her heart was in her throat, she nodded. But as the beautiful yellow diamond slid into place on her left hand, Adelaide recovered enough to fling her arms around him.

"I love you more than anything, too. And that was my favorite proposal yet." Her voice was all wobbly, along with the rest of her.

Her big, strong future husband lifted her off her feet and pressed his lips to hers, his arms banded around her waist. He took his time with the kiss, making up for the days and nights they'd missed each other. Heat tingled over her skin, awakening every part of her. She was breathless and a little light-headed by the time he broke contact.

"I meant it as a compliment that I wanted you to be on my team." He smiled up at her and she laughed.

"I am complimented." Her heart swelled with love for him. She bracketed his face in her hands while he carried her into her bedroom. "But thank you for letting me be more than that."

"I'm going to be the best husband you can imagine," he promised, his golden-brown eyes dazzling her more than either of the rings on her fingers.

"I'm going to remind you every day that I love you," she promised him in return, her body sinking into the bed as Dempsey laid her down.

He stretched out next to her, his muscular frame filling her small bed so that he crowded her in the most delicious ways.

"I'd like to start now, by adoring every inch of you." His words were warm on her neck as he kissed that vulnerable spot.

"That's perfect, because every inch of me has missed you." She trailed a hand through his dark hair, knowing she was the luckiest woman on earth.

Her fairy tale hadn't ended. The best part was just beginning.

* * * * *

COMING NEXT MONTH FROM

HARLEQUIN
Desire

Available April 5, 2016

#2437 TAKE ME, COWBOY
Copper Ridge • by Maisey Yates
Tomboy Anna Brown *wants* to tap into her femininity, but is clueless on *how* to do so. When her brothers bet she'll be dateless at a charity auction, she turns to a makeover—and her way-too-sexy best friend—to prove them wrong.

#2438 HIS BABY AGENDA
Billionaires and Babies • by Katherine Garbera
Gabi De La Cruz thought she'd found Mr. Right...until he was arrested for murder! Now he's back and needs help with his young child, but is there room for a second chance when he's obsessed with clearing his name?

#2439 A SURPRISE FOR THE SHEIKH
Texas Cattleman's Club: Lies and Lullabies
by Sarah M. Anderson
Sheikh Rafe bin Saleed wants revenge, and he'll buy Royal, Texas, to get it. But will a night of unplanned passion with his enemy's sister give him a baby he didn't bargain for?

#2440 A BARGAIN WITH THE BOSS
Chicago Sons • by Barbara Dunlop
Playboy brother Tucker has no desire to run the family corporation, but a scandal forces his hand. His trial by fire heats up even more when he clashes with the feisty, sexy secretary who's hiding a big secret from him...

#2441 REUNITED WITH THE REBEL BILLIONAIRE
Bayou Billionaires • by Catherine Mann
After being ordered to reunite with his estranged wife to keep his career stable, a football superstar realizes that their fake relationship is more than an assignment. It might be what he wants more than anything else...

#2442 SECRET CHILD, ROYAL SCANDAL
The Sherdana Royals • by Cat Schield
Marrying his former lover to legitimize his secret son's claim to the throne becomes more challenging than prince Christian Alessandro expected. Because Noelle Dubonne makes a demand of her own—it's true love or nothing!

---

*Tomboy Anna Brown wants to tap into her femininity,
but is clueless on how to do so. When her brothers bet
she'll be dateless at a charity auction, she turns to a
makeover—and her way-too-sexy best friend—to prove
them wrong.*

Read on for a sneak peek at
TAKE ME, COWBOY,
the latest in USA TODAY *bestselling author*
Maisey Yates's *COPPER RIDGE series*

Anna dropped the towel and unzipped the bag, staring at
the contents with no small amount of horror. There was…
underwear inside it. Underwear that Chase had purchased
for her for their first fake date. She grabbed the pair of
panties that were attached to a little hanger. Oh, they had
no back. She supposed guessing her size didn't matter
much. She swallowed hard, rubbing her thumb over
the soft material. He would know exactly what she was
wearing beneath the dress. Would know just how little
that was.

*He isn't going to think about it. Because he doesn't
think about you that way.*

He never had. He never would. She was never going
to touch him, either. She'd made that decision a long time
ago. For a lot of reasons that were as valid today as they
had been the very first time he'd ever made her stomach
jump when she looked at him.

She tugged on the clothes, having to do a pretty intense
wiggle to get the slinky red dress up all the way before

zipping it into place. She took a deep breath, turned around. She faced her reflection in the mirror full-on. She looked… Well, her hair was wet and straggly, and she looked half-drowned. She didn't look curvy, or shimmery, or delightful. She sighed heavily, trying to ignore the sinking feeling in her stomach.

Chase really was going to have to be a miracle worker in order to pull this off.

"Buck up," she said to herself.

So what was one more moment of feeling inadequate? Honestly, in the broad tapestry of her life it would barely register. She was never quite what was expected. She never quite fit. So why'd she expect that she was going to put on a sexy dress and suddenly be transformed into the kind of sex kitten she didn't even want to be?

She gritted her teeth, throwing open the bedroom door and walking into the room. "I hope you're happy," she said, flinging her arms wide. "You get what you get."

Chase, who had been completely silent upon her entry into the room, remained so. She glared at him. He wasn't saying anything. He was only staring. "Well?"

"It's nice," he said.

His voice sounded rough, and kind of thin.

"You're a liar."

"I'm not a liar."

"Are you satisfied?" she asked.

His jaw tensed, a muscle in his cheek ticking. "I guess you could say that."

Whatever You're Into… Passionate Reads

Looking for more passionate reads from Harlequin®?
Fear not! Harlequin® Presents, Harlequin® Desire and
Harlequin® Blaze offer you irresistible romance stories
featuring powerful heroes.

HARLEQUIN *Presents*

Do you want alpha males, decadent glamour and jet-set
lifestyles? Step into the sensational, sophisticated world of
Harlequin® Presents, where sinfully tempting heroes ignite a
fierce and wickedly irresistible passion!

HARLEQUIN *Desire*

Harlequin® Desire novels are powerful, passionate and
provocative contemporary romances set against a backdrop of
wealth, privilege and sweeping family saga. Alpha heroes with
a soft side meet strong-willed but vulnerable heroines amid a
dramatic world of divided loyalties, high-stakes conflict and
intense emotion.

HARLEQUIN *Blaze*

Harlequin® Blaze stories sizzle with strong heroines and
irresistible heroes playing the game of modern love and lust.
They're fun, sexy and always steamy.

Be sure to check out our full selection of books
within each series every month!

www.Harlequin.com